Chapter 1

It was bitterly cold. The type of cold that Sgt. Binks wished he was reading about in a book, instead of experiencing. Sgt. Binks imagined himself, with such a book in hand, sitting next to a crackling fireplace with a hot cup of cocoa on a stand next to him.

Sgt. Binks imagined these things to himself as he marched slowly along the snow-covered Korean landscape. He was plodding along on what was once a dirt road but was now effectively a path of ice that jutted up and dropped down unevenly, reflecting the deep tire ruts in the road that was now covered in a sheet of compressed snow and ice. He often found that his mind wandered to these fantasy lands of warmth and cocoa during these monotonous marches toward the front line.

In this daydream, he imagined that the fire would be crackling and popping, and his feet would be propped up while he would be thinking about how it's almost too hot…being so close to the fire. It was hard to stay in the daydream when the sub-freezing winds were whipping snow into your face.

Every gust of wind was a brutal reminder of where they were, and every exhale and its' vapor that rose in front of your face was impossible to ignore. It was far below freezing. The type of weather that makes you forget about anything else but the temperature. The entire world was one giant freezer that made you forget about any inhibitions you may have ever had about curling up next to another man to stay warm at night.

When it's that cold, sounds travel farther. The silence of everything surrounding the column of Marines accentuated the sounds that the column made. It was a blanket of extreme silence that was punctured by the noise of a reinforced battalion marching on hard frozen earth. It was peaceful when you looked in the right direction at the right time. It was possible that one would see nothing but rolling hills covered in white snow with the occasional trees. It looked like the type of beautiful landscape you would see in a painting. The blanket of snow enveloped all the imperfections of the surrounding terrain.

Inevitably though, some loud noise would cut through the silence and your head would involuntarily shift from the beauty of the land to where the noise had come from. Reality would flood back and Sgt. Binks spirit would be dragged back to the darkness it had been lifted from. The noise could have been any number of things; the clanging of the metal-fuel jugs strapped to the outside of a military vehicle, a gunshot, or an explosion. The noise would sometimes come from the mouth of a Marine who would curse because he had just tripped on the uneven ice-covered road they were marching down.

Sometimes, the stumbling Marine would fall onto the ground and when that happened, it was a funny thing to see. They would tip over like a statue, due to the amount of clothing and gear they had layered on to try to stay warm. The statue would fall while cursing with the ferocity of the devil and the vocal cords of a bulldog. Sgt. Binks's lips turned up ever so slightly at the corners when he imagined the image of a half bulldog half human being. Not so much that any civilian or any stranger to the man would even have the slightest clue he was amused, but they did move. Which may as well have been a bellowing laugh from any other man, so rare it was to see any emotion on his gaunt face.

The sensation of the smile felt odd to Sgt. Binks. He hadn't smiled in some time. All the Marines in Korea were miserable, a fact that was a source of amusement from time to time. This shared misery was the fire from which the iron bond of combat units was forged in.

It made you feel like you had a family with you, going through the same thing. Suffering by yourself can be one of the worst things in the world. Suffering with good companions can be amusing despite the pain, and many lifelong friendships were born from that shared suffering.

It was so frigid that Sgt. Binks didn't have as much hate for the Motor-t officers as he usually did, given that there was nowhere for them to hide from the torturous cold. They were assaulted by the cold just like the rest of the Marines. The heaters in almost all of the vehicles were terrible and the amount of heat they generated wasn't even enough to compensate for the fact that you were sitting down and not moving to generate body heat.

In addition to that, by this point in the march, almost none of the vehicles had windows anymore. Most had been shot out by the enemy. The vehicles made good targets and behind those vehicles is where the infantry would try to find cover from attacks, and as such (whether the intended victims were the vehicles or the infantry) the vehicles always ended up taking fire any time there was contact with the enemy.

Sgt. Binks had been admiring the beauty of the frosty countryside when a noise had turned his attention back to the column of Marines marching down the road. A Marine had tripped on a frozen dirt clod and had spewed vehement obscenities while falling into the middle of the road. Sgt. Binks went over to the source of the noise, a fellow Marine of his platoon, and offered his hand. The cursing Marine took the offered hand and stood up.

"Thanks," the Marine said.

Sgt. Binks looked at the Marines rifle and saw that some dirt and snow had been packed into the barrel after the Marine had fallen.

"You got a little bit of dirt in the barrel," he said pointing to it.

Smith unslung his rifle from his shoulder and examined the damage and, then, with a slight tone of irritation remarked "Son of a…" as he attempted to clean it as best as possible without taking his gloves off.

"I got a little bit of tape if you want to tape over it. It might help you keep it clean. You want some?" Binks asked.

"Yeah. Sure." Smith replied, then added a "Thanks." as Binks searched for his tape.

Binks reached into his right coat pocket on the exterior of his coat and fumbled around until he could tell which object was the roll of tape, and then, pulled it out and gave it to his fellow Marine. Smith took the tape and began to try to apply it while they were walking down the road, in trace of the company jeep. Smith attempted to deal with the tape without having to take his gloves off, but it was quickly proving to be a futile task.

Binks saw Smith fumble with the venture of tearing off a piece of tape while wearing gloves that made his hands three times larger than they normally were and he reached his hand out again and said "Give it here."

Smith handed it over and began to mumble something about how it was practically impossible to do anything with these damned gloves on and how it was too cold to take them off. Binks clamped his teeth onto the end of the index finger on his glove and tugged his hand out of it, then he tucked the glove under his left armpit and squeezed his left elbow tight to his body to make sure the glove stayed in place as they continued to walk.

Binks fumbled with the tape until he found the end of it and then dug under it with his fingernail so he could grab a hold of it with his teeth. His teeth held the end while he pulled the roll of tape away from his body until he had about three inches unrolled.

"Lemme see it," Sgt. Binks said while indicating that Smith should show him the muzzle of his rifle. Smith unslung his BAR (Browning Automatic Rifle) and held it an angle so that Binks could apply the tape, which he did in a hurry. He tugged his glove back onto his right hand and readjusted his M1 Garand that had begun to slip off his shoulder while he had been otherwise occupied.

"Cold as hell!" Binks said with frustration and anger laced in his voice.

Smith smirked and added to Binks mild-mannered tirade by saying, "Yeah, should have joined the fuckin' Air Force."

Binks nodded his agreement, but inside he knew that was never really something he wanted. He wanted to be on the ground facing the enemy, not a mechanic or behind a desk in the Air Force, as nice as the idea sounded in that moment.

They continued to walk side by side in silence. Binks thoughts drifted. He stared ahead into the distance and didn't focus on any one thing in particular, but instead just let his eyes wander for a few minutes. After a while, he watched the vapor from his breath as he exhaled.

It's too cold, he thought to himself. The last he had heard someone report the temperature, it was 10 degrees. It was probably a little below that now. When you accounted for the added cold from the wind, it was probably closer to 0 degrees. His breath expanded out in front of him and upwards as it slowly dissipated and was replaced with an identical cloud with the next breath that left his body. He thought for a moment about how amazing the human body was to be able to survive in such an abominable climate.

Binks glanced to his right at Cpl. Smith and began to think about the things that he knew about him to find something they might talk about to pass the time. Smith was suffering. The weather, along with so many other things associated with a war, was beginning to get to Smith. Binks thought he might try to distract him from the fact that they were walking in some god-forsaken weather in the middle of nowhere just hoping for a fight with the enemy to break the routine of everyday life. Sgt. Binks remembered that Smith was from Texas.

"What's Texas like this time of year?" Binks asked looking over at Smith to see if he heard or registered the fact that he had been spoken to. Smith looked up and made eye contact with Binks showing he had heard him. Binks raised his eyebrows to reiterate through body language that he was waiting on a response and then Smith stumbled and was on his way down again, just as the words were starting to come out.

"Honestly, it's prob--" Smith started to say and then he tripped on another frozen dirt clod and began his statuesque fall towards the earth for the second time and the sentence changed to, "fuck!"

Binks reached down and offered his hand once again and glanced down at Smiths' BAR as he did so and noticed that the tape he had applied was still in place. Some dirt was on the tape but none of the snow had gotten inside the barrel this time.

"At least there is nothing in your gun this time," Binks offered in an attempt to raise Smiths' spirit as he pulled his fellow Marine up.

Smith stood up and readjusted his BAR and mumbled his thanks as they made their way again in trace of the jeep with their company commander, Captain Gordon.

"It's probably raining in Texas," Smith said, in response to Binks's question. "So it would still be shit weather, but at least I'd be around the fireplace, or at a bar somewhere…definitely wouldn't be walkin' 20 fuckin miles in it."

"Rain a lot in Texas? You're from Loredo right?" Binks asked.

"Yeah, where are you from?"

"Kentucky. From a small farm in Lone Oak, Kentucky."

"What kind of farm?"

"We just grew hay, alfalfa rich hay. Just 20 acres."

"You got a girl back home?"

"Kinda, I got a girl I write letters to…I don't know yet if anything will come of it." Binks answered.

"Yeah?" Smith asked, encouraging him to continue.

"Yeah," Binks said, "I'm gonna check up on the guys real quick."

Binks turned around and stood in the middle of the road. Marines continued to walk by on either side with roughly five meters between each one. They marched in this manner so that no one incoming mortar or artillery shell could take out more than a few Marines at a time. He checked off mentally that all 12 of his Marines were accounted for.

Sgt Binks counted as every one of the 12 Marines in his section walked by, nodding to the team leaders and visually inspecting the Marines, looking to see if anything was out of the ordinary. Then he walked back up to Cpl. Smith who was the first team leader for the section as well as Sgt. Binks's 2nd in command. If Sgt Binks died or became a casualty then Cpl. Smith would assume command of the section.

Sgt. Binks oversaw three teams. Within each team there was a gunner, two assistant gunners, and a team leader. The gunners and assistant gunners carried an M1 Garand and the team leader carried a BAR. They rotated carrying all the parts of a M20, a 75mm recoilless rifle, capable of firing anti-armor rounds or anti-personnel rounds. The M20 was a beast of a weapon that could reach 3.9 miles at its maximum range and could penetrate up to 100mm of armor with its High Explosive Anti-Tank round. With the heavy power of the M20 came the responsibility of transporting the 103 lbs. weapon, and its accompanying 53 lbs. tripod. It was not typical that the team leaders carried the BAR, but Sgt. Binks had it set up that way in his section because the BAR was important in firefights, and he needed the people he could trust the most with controlling the automatic fire. Binks himself, carried a M1 Garand rifle and a M1911 sidearm.

Binks reached into the inside of his jacket and grabbed a package of crackers, broke off a piece, and then put the package back. He chewed the dry cracker slowly and went back to scanning the surrounding landscape. The cracker was flavorless. It provided little benefit other than to slightly dull the gnawing hunger and temporarily take his mind off things as he focused solely on not choking from the dryness of it. He had been in Korea for only a few weeks but he felt like he had walked enough to have made it through all of China by now. The days were filled with walking and digging defensive perimeters and the nights were filled with jumping into those fox holes or "fighting holes" and taking turns standing watch. The column halted. He glanced up the road to see what was going on, but the front of the battalion was too far ahead for him to see so he just turned around and looked for Smith.

"Cpl. Smith, set in security over there with your team until we start moving again." Sgt. Binks said, while pointing to a mound that was slightly elevated about 50 meters off the left-hand side of the road, that offered a better vantage point of the surrounding area.

"Roger that." Smith offered his two-word response and then motioned to the three other members of his team to follow him as he started towards the elevated ground. Sgt. Binks walked back down to his other teams while at the same time motioning for them to come to him. Cpl. Jones and Cpl. Williams, the other two team leaders in the section walked towards him.

"What's happening?" Cpl. Jones asked. Jones was another great leader in the section and was third in the chain of command and would be in charge if both Sgt. Binks and Cpl. Smith was taken out of action.

Jones was a tall and lanky fellow, with a deep permanent scowl, who looked like he was always ready to fight.

"Not quite sure, it's almost 1500 so we may be digging in here for the night. But honestly, I don't know. Post your guys on the left-hand side of the road and if we are here longer than an hour, you will relieve first team on over-watch. Williams: post your guys on the right side, rotate with Jones for over-watch if we are still here at 1700. Let's just run at 50% security." Binks finished and then glanced at the two to see if there were any more questions.

"Roger that" and "Ok" were the two responses from Williams and Jones respectively.

"I will go check in with the LT and see what's up, I'll let you know as soon as I get any word." Binks said and then turned and made his way up the road towards the company jeep, where his platoon commander was riding with the company commander. The platoon commander was also acting as the company Executive Officer, since the previous one had been shot in the head earlier that day. About 9 miles of walking ago.

As he walked, Binks looked to his left to see how the first team was doing on overwatch and saw that Smith had just finished setting everyone in, and they appeared to be appropriately covering sectors to the north and the west that was not visible from where Binks was on the road.

He had been blessed by the infantry gods to have such great team leaders. Lord knows that half the Non-Commissioned Officers in this company seem to be barely competent enough to walk a straight line and somehow Binks had landed three NCOs that would be listed among the best he had ever worked with.

Binks blew a kiss to the sky along with a prayer of thanks. He sent it up to whatever entity may be listening, to show his love and appreciation for this blessing and then turned his gaze back to the company jeep. The LT was talking with Gunny Mckinley. As Binks walked up, they finished their conversation and the LT turned and headed back to the jeep, leaving the Gunny by himself.

"Good Afternoon Gunny," Binks said, offering the proper greeting of the day, and then waited to be addressed. Gunny Mckinley nodded his acknowledgment of the greeting and then immediately started passing on the information he had just been briefed on by the Lieutenant.

"The Army is getting hit by the Chinese across the other side of a reservoir a few miles up," he said pointing to the Northeast "and I don't know for sure but we may be assigned to help support them, situation depending. As of right now the plan is still to head North," he said pointing farther down the road they were on "and reinforce the Marines that have caught hell last night near Yudam-Ni. They need some replacements. Right now they are getting a dead truck out of the road, then we will move about two more miles today and then set in for the night…so tell your boys not to get too comfortable right now and just post up security till we start moving again."

"Roger that," Binks said and then turned and headed back to his section.

The machine-gun section leader was on his way up and Binks relayed what he had just been told by Gunny Mckinley. They stayed in position for about 20 more minutes before picking up again. Binks motioned to the first team to fall back into the column and watched as Smith gathered his Marines and jogged back to the road.

"That was a pretty good position up there. Would be a defensive dream, practically no dead space." Smith remarked as he fell back into the column opposite of Binks.

"Oh yeah? Good." Binks replied, somewhat absent-mindedly, and then added "We may be making some pretty strong contact tonight, make sure your guys keep a good lookout. If not tonight then probably tomorrow, but soon."

"Yeah, I already told them, but I will make sure it happens." Smith paused then adjusted his coat and said "it's so goddam cold." while shaking his head in frustration. The two men walked in silence until they stopped again about an hour later and the word was passed back that this was where they would be setting in for the night. The companies were assigned areas to dig in and defend in the event of an attack.

It was early evening and the sun was hanging above a mountain range to the west, about an hour away from dipping out of sight. Binks walked down the line and checked up on his team leaders and their teams before dropping onto the ground with his back against an embankment and his face towards the sunset. The wind was starting to pick up a little bit, as it had been for the last couple of weeks around this time in the evening, and he pulled the collar of his jacket up a little bit and tucked his jaw down to his chest to shield his face as much as possible from the wind. He stared out over the landscape before him and followed the silhouette of the mountain range with his eyes. It looked so similar to the Northern Rockies in the wintertime that it was easy to forget for a moment exactly where you were.

The way that the brutally cold winds hit your face and the manner in which the dry air you're your eyes water was no different than the way it had felt when he had gone hunting as a child. When you pause at the top of a hill and breathe as quietly as possible and try to listen and look for any sign of movement or any noise that might indicate the presence or passing of your intended prey. Moments like those, you just focus on your senses and try to interpret what your body is telling you about the world around you.

You focus on what your ears can tell you from the sounds, and what your eyes can tell you from the way that they pick up the light around you, what your nose can tell you from the smells that drift to it on the wind, and what your skin can tell you about the way that the wind blows. Those moments when you do nothing but focus on your senses were special. Here in Korea for a second, you would forget where you were.

Binks thought back to when he was a child and read in the history books about the great battles that were fought and wars that were won. The conquerors that conquered in their times: and the way that those stories had played out in his mind. The men in those stories were always made of something more than the flesh and bone that was common to mankind in Binks' childhood imagination. Those men had possessed something that he could never attain. The battles they had fought in were in different times and in different places than what Binks ever imagined he would see in his lifetime.

He was one of those men now. History would not soon forget this war, and he now had a role in it. Sgt. Binks looked out over the Korean landscape and saw that the war zone that he now occupied was filled with the same wind, and the same smell, and the same noise that he felt as a child while hunting in snow-covered mountains. His bones were the same, and he felt the same as he did then, only more experienced. He felt oddly out of place. Like a kid sitting at the grown-up table during Thanksgiving. Despite feeling his youth still present in his body, he was part of what would undoubtedly be written about in the history books. Part of a war that may shape the future of the world and part of the greatest fighting force known to mankind. He was a young boy in a grown man's body that had the responsibility of fighting in this war.

That's what made these moments so surreal for Binks. The realization that the wars that he had read and romanticized about as a child, he was now a part of. He had become his childhood hero in many ways…and yet he felt no different. The cold wind still bit at his unprotected cheeks in the same way it had in the mountains he had hunted as a boy. The clanking of metal on metal still sounded the same as when they would load the truck up with firewood from an expedition into the forest and strap the extra metal gas to the side with the saws.

The gun smoke smelled the same in the cold air after you pulled the trigger, only now there were men on the other side of the muzzle and not elk or deer. It was interesting how at this moment, those same senses and feelings were not isolated to where he was, and not associated with war at all.

The memory of the company Executive Officer getting killed earlier that day returned to Binks and he felt sick to think about how the man had no way of knowing when his last-second would be. One second the officer was a man who loved his family and cared about his Marines and then in the very next second he was a lifeless lump of bones and meat with no more love of family or adherence to a life of duty than a rock.

A movement in the corner of his eye drew Sgt. Binks from his thoughts and back to the real world where he adjusted his eyes accordingly to fixate on the object that had drawn his attention. It was Gunny Mckinley walking towards him. Binks posted out on his right hand and shifted his hips so that he was in a three-point stance of sorts with his left hand on his rifle sling and his right on the ground and his toes on both feet, and then he pushed off the hill with his hand and stood to meet the Gunny. Standing up with all the cold weather clothes and gear on was an ordeal every time.

"Evening Gunny." He said offering the formal proper greeting of the day, as was Binks manner.

He was answered by the informal greeting of "Binks!" and a slap on the shoulder "How are you and your boys holding up?"

"Good Gunny…You want me to pick where to set my guys in or do you have something in mind?"

"What were you thinking?"

"Well, I doubt we have much of a threat coming from the east. I'd post them with first and 2nd on the west side of the road and 3rd on the east with the main objective being to cover the road since that's the most likely place we will cross enemy approach…and if we get hit from somewhere else we will displace and go to wherever the threat is, but I don't think there's much chance of needing them anywhere other than the road."

Binks looked at the Gunny to see what he thought and saw that he was nodding in agreement.

"All right, get to it then."

"Roger that Gunny," Binks said and then turned and motioned for the team leaders.

Chapter 2

Binks set the teams in and made sure that they had a clear view of the road. He set out markers to ensure the distances between them and any oncoming attacks would already have been ranged appropriately so that the rounds they fired would be accurate. This also helped with calling in fire missions from air support or mortars through a radio. He set himself in with the first team for the night on the West side of the road.

Sgt. Binks walked up as his teams were beginning to dig their fighting holes and broke out his e-tool and started to help. The ground was frozen, and hard to break into and they had to work at a fast pace to get the holes dug before the sun went down. Every time a Marine would swing his e-tool, with the full weight of his body behind it, a depressingly small amount of frozen dirt and ice would become dislodged.

It was a tiring and frustrating business. It had been a new defensive position every day for the last three days and the experience every time was maddeningly similar in how long and how much effort it took to dig the positions. One Marine stayed on security watching the horizon and they rotated every five minutes so that every 15 minutes one of the members of the first team would have five minutes of rest. Binks didn't take a break but instead continued to work tirelessly to help dig the hole.

By the time the sun was setting they had a hole about five feet deep, and about six feet wide at its widest. It was intended for two men but Binks squeezed in, and no one complained. Even though there was less space with three Marines in the hole it would help to keep them warm, and warmth took precedence over concern for space in the Marines' minds. Binks left the first team and went to check up on the others. The other teams fighting holes were not as deep or as well done, but they were adequate to provide shelter from the wind and enemy fire, and as such he didn't make them dig further. Binks slid back into the hole with the first team and offered to take the first watch while the others got out their Down sleeping bags and cocooned themselves inside of them. Binks was once again left with his thoughts and the quiet world around him.

He always offered to take the first watch because he would rather have to stay up an extra few hours longer than have an interrupted sleep pattern at night. Nobody got more than six hours a night and he preferred to get those six in a row rather than two hours and then four or four hours and then two. The first or last watch was always the best, in his opinion. He pointed his rifle out across the land in front of their position and then allowed his mind to wander as his eyes methodically pierced the darkness left to right, then right to left.

He thought about many different things while on watch. He imagined seeing the Chinese attacking. He imagined shooting while yelling the location of the enemy to the others who would be just waking up.

Giving them the direction and range so that his fellow Marines would know where to look. He imagined seeing a cluster of them behind a boulder about 250 meters out and having the 75mm recoilless rifles fire at them and send them flying into the air.

He thought about what he would do if a Marine nearby was injured. Sgt. Binks spent a few moments running through mentally what to do in each of the main situations he might encounter. What to do if the casualty had been shot in an artery and what to do if a lung had been hit, or if their spine was hurt. What to do with compound fractures, flesh wounds, how to stop arterial bleeding. After he had run through those things in his mind and was sure that he was ready for anything that might come his way while he was on watch, he allowed his mind to wander to other things while his eyes continued to pry into the darkness for anything that might be a threat.

He thought about the girl back home. The last letter he had gotten from her was from an airdrop to the ship when they were on their way to Korea. She had sent him letters for the past year or so off and on. He had kept a few of them tucked into a little notebook he kept in his left breast pocket and would take out and read from time to time. It felt good to know that someone cared enough to write him a letter longhand like that, and so when he didn't have time to re-read the letters, he would just think about it and touch the notebook. The simple act of feeling the letters always brought a modicum of light back into his otherwise darkened mind.

She was a young girl. She was innocent and her innocence showed in her letters and made them all the sweeter to read. The two of them were not in love, not him with her or her with him, but the letters were written with love. A sort of loving empathy, not the sort of love that makes you ache to hold the person you think about but the love of someone who cares enough about what you are doing and where you are to try to comfort you. Binks liked the letters.

As he stared out over the Korean landscape his mind drifted from thoughts of the girl back home to thoughts about where he was now. In a war. A game with the most serious of consequences, death. He thought about how he had watched the Company Executive Officer slump down after he had been shot in the head. The man had collapsed into a lifeless clump of mass that was devoid of all hopes and dreams for the future. He had been robbed of those dreams by the bullet.

Such a small thing, a bullet. A bullet that had been shot by a person that may have had no personal ill will towards the Executive Officer. The sniper had squeezed his trigger, then he saw his target drop. With just the movement of a finger, he had taken a father from his kids, a brother from his siblings, a son from his family, an officer from his men, and a husband from his wife.

Binks reflected on the beauty of life and how the things that seem so normal when they happen are the most abnormal. How sometimes it seemed that all humans were evil and yet there are a few heavenly moments, such as when a child laughs, that the world is not so evil. He considered the ocean and the powerful waves that could be a man's worst enemy and yet no one would argue their beauty while observing from afar while dry and safe.

He ruminated on the things in nature that could kill a man. A waterfall, white water rapids, fire, cold, and predators in their natural habitat…almost everything could kill you, but we call the deadliest of them 'beautiful' when we are not in the middle of its destruction. How quickly the wind could shift from one way to the other, or how the sunlight could vanish behind a cloud, how rain changed to hail, and then back to rain, how lighting strikes and then disappears all without a thought for the lives it takes when it does.

Some things just were a certain way, and that was their nature. Was war just human nature? Do we fight and kill with the illusion that we have a choice when in reality we have no more choice than the wind does over whether it blows or not? He looked at his gloved hand wrapped around the stock of his rifle and wondered if the true and ultimate utility of it was to be used as a weapon in war.

He thought about his dad and how as a kid he would help him with projects around the house. They would be working to fix something and Binks would be holding a piece of wood up to the wall while his dad turned the screwdriver. Binks remembered looking at those hands that turned the screwdriver and seeing how massive they were in comparison to his own hands. They were enormous to him as a child and were ingrained in his memory in that way.

His father's hands were formed from working all his life in the way that he had known best, with sweat on his brow and a tool in his hand and a clear task in front of him to accomplish. That feeling of accomplishing a task is very rewarding and that rewarding feeling is the understandable allure of working in manual labor. To finish something and look at the tangible results of your labor and be proud of your handiwork. Binks had never spent much time thinking about his dad until he had come to Korea. It seemed that his father was on his mind quite often when Binks was on watch. Staring out across open land for hours on end often leads to an intense introspective evaluation of human life, and many things that had never crossed his mind seemed to pop up out of nowhere.

Whenever he thought of his dad he thought of his hands. His dad had never said "Look at my hands, these are the hands of a hardworking man" and yet when Binks thought of his dad, he couldn't help but think of his hands. The hands of Binks' father told a story of their own. They were darker than the rest of his body by several shades from the work done in the sun while in long sleeve shirts. Darker than his face that was shaded from the sun by the worn-out hat he often wore.

Most times that Binks saw those hands was when he was holding a board that the hands were nailing down, or supporting a car part that was being tightened back up, or passing those hands a bale of hay from the field during harvest or an irrigation pipe during the springtime, or river rocks for the landscaping, lumber for construction, wood for splitting or that he had just split, or the right sized wrench or nut or bolt…and as such his hands and those hands of his dads were nearly always dirty.

Binks knew the type of labor that went into dirty hands, and there was a difference between freshly muddied hands and hands that had been dirty for the last 12 hours, in which case the skin itself seemed to have absorbed and adopted the same sort of color as the dirt or oil they were covered in. Binks saw that the hands of his dad were always covered in dirt and oil by the time he got home from work in the way that hands often were when they were engaged in hard dirty work for the whole day. Bink's dad never really talked about work…or about anything really, and Binks himself was a quiet kid and never asked but had observed the evidence that pointed to the conclusion that his dad worked hard every day.

Binks knew that this was the mark of a good man. He had never been consciously aware of it before, but as Binks thought about his dad he realized that he had probably seen more of his father's hands than of his face. His father's hands were a reflection of who he was and what he had spent his whole life doing. He thought about his own hands and hands in general. Hands never lie. A man may say that he is tough, or that he has worked hard in the fields, but his soft hands would betray this delusion. A working man's hands will contract when he is relaxed because that is their natural state having been used so long to grab, lift, hold, pull, push, grip, clutch, grasp, and clench all manner of tools and materials.

Binks father had hands that were rough as sandpaper from callouses from the work they had done. Hard work builds a tough man and hands like those can only be crafted through hard work. Binks pulled his watch out of his pocket and was able to tell, by the light of the moon, that an hour had passed since he had assumed watch. One more hour and then he was done.

He glanced over at the other Marines in the hole and noticed that Smith's head had shifted in his sleep so that it now rested on the barrel of his BAR. Binks reached over and gently pushed on the right side of Smiths' head until it flopped over and away from the muzzle, then he took his right glove off and keeping his eyes on the terrain in front of him he followed the barrel down with his fingers until they came upon the safety selector for the weapon, whereupon he felt to make sure it was in the safe position. He pulled his glove back on and returned to looking out over the endless white snow before him and mentally ran through what to do in the event of an attack once again.

The moon was only a little more than half full but even the partial reflection of the light on the snow made it easy to see for several hundred yards. The moon had been full when they had first landed in Korea and he recalled how at that first night it had been so bright that you could see everything very clearly over an open field. Binks readjusted his clothing and leaned back and allowed his mind to wander once again while staying vigilant with his eyes on the land in front of him.

He wondered what life would be like after this war was over. He didn't imagine this could last much longer. Perhaps a month or so he thought. Then what would come next? He still had another three years left of service. Would it be nothing but training for three years? Maybe he would re-enlist.

Binks wondered what his family would say when he got home from the war. He could see himself at a bar after the war and the old fellows there that fought in WW1 would offer to buy him a round of whiskey and the women perhaps would be curious of what it would be like to be the lover of a man who had just returned from war. Then he thought about the girl that wrote him the letters again and pondered if he would ever see her again or if she existed only in her letters and the fantasies that he had when he dreamt of her.

He remembered her face and how when she sat on his lap one night his body had responded to her presence in a way that would have been embarrassing for him had she stood up and his friends around the bonfire would have seen it. He remembered her looking at him with a twinkle in her eye and leaning in and whispering, about how she could feel him. He had been a shy boy and didn't know how to respond in that situation, so nothing ever came of it. They had stayed friends, but now they had been writing for almost a year back and forth and he was hoping that when he went back, she would go back to the way she was before. He thought back again to her sitting on his lap and his mind took him through his memories to that place and his body responded to those thoughts. Binks found that it was always easier to stay awake on a post late at night when thinking about such things.

It was, in fact, the key to staying awake. To think about sex to the point that it becomes painful was a balancing act between fantastical fictional pleasure and a very real aching for sexual release. He could be exhausted, but as long as he could focus on sex, he could stay awake. It was a well-developed talent that was forced into formation by the lack of female companionship and the need to stay awake. These types of thoughts helped many a Marine stay awake on late-night watch and kept many alive as a consequence. Binks pushed his hips forward to where they were firmly pressed against the front on the fighting hole and imagined the pressure came the girl sitting on his lap again and not from the frozen Korean dirt. He stared out over the snow in front of him and dreamed with his eyes open, his mind now an inferno of sexual imagination.

Binks took his watch out and looked at the time. There was five minutes left on his shift of post.

He got out his sleeping bag and began unlacing his boots while keeping an eye on security. The bootlaces were frozen, and his hands were cold. He reached over and flicked Smiths' ear and then went back to untying his boots. Smith made a quiet and low growling noise like a dog makes when you approach him while he is eating his food, and then Smith slowly sat up and began to find his socks and pull them onto his feet while remaining in his bag. Smith stepped out of his bag and slid his feet into his boots and began adjusting his clothing that had been bunched up during his two hours of sleep.

Smith slung his weapon and then looked over at Binks crawling into his sleeping bag and said in a whisper that carried perfectly in the cold night air…

"Fuck this place."

Binks smirked, pulled his rifle close, shut his eyes, and immediately fell asleep.

Chapter 3

Sgt Binks woke to the sound of an engine sputtering to life in the Korean cold. He felt his face and the stubble on it and knew he would have to shave today, despite how cold it was. He thought about how someday it would be nice to have a beard and to have hair so long and thick that it was like the mane of a lion. To wake up and go to sleep whenever he wanted to, and not at the whim of his superiors or the enemy. He stood up and mentally added sleeping in a warm bed to the list of things he couldn't wait to do when this war was over. That would be heavenly.

He packed his sleeping bag and slung his pack and rifle and then checked in with the other teams to see how their night was and tell them to start filling in the fighting holes and get ready to move out. The battalion moved forward at around 0800 and Binks checked to make sure the whole section was accounted for before moving back to his usual position in the marching column, opposite of Smith. They walked for a couple of hours before arriving at the location they were to defend. Other battalions were already getting hammered by the Chinese on either side of them and they were to hold this position so that the Chinese would not be able to punch through the middle and surround them.

Binks was given orders and told to set up a blocking position with his section on a road leading towards the regimental aid station. Binks positioned his men with the first team on the west side of the road and 2nd and 3rd on the east and had them begin digging in and fortifying their positions. It was early afternoon when they began to dig and the sounds of sporadic gunfire and the occasional explosion drifted to them from somewhere off to the left of their position.

Binks worked with Smith to ensure that the process of digging went as quickly as possible. The sounds of firing that were drifting to them from the west were only a few potshots every few minutes and they were only barely distinguishable. The sky was clear and as such the air support was strong since the pilots had good visibility and the sounds of them flying overhead and dropping payloads on the enemy were becoming an increasingly common thing.

Two Marines were helping a casualty down from the hill to the west. The casualty had suffered a bullet wound to his right leg and was hopping on his left leg while the Marines on either side of him assisted with his weight as he hopped down the hill. They came to a stop next to where Binks and his men were digging in and they asked if anyone had cigarettes while they took a short break since the aid station was still another 300 yards back behind the line. Binks reached inside his jacket with his left hand and fumbled around for a package of cigarettes that was already partially destroyed, but the sticks themselves remained intact for the most part and could still be smoked.

"Here." Binks stretched his hand out with the package in them and the first Marine grabbed it, took three, and then handed it back to Binks. His name tape read OBRIAN in all capital letters and Binks wondered if there was supposed to be an apostrophe after the O but the name tags didn't reflect that. The military was never the place for proper spelling. Obrian looked at the molested cigarettes and smirked at the sight of them and the fact that even the cigarettes looked like they were war-torn and tattered.

"Much obliged." The Marine said and then handed one of the cigarettes to the 2nd able-bodied Marine and the other cigarette to the injured Marine who was more than willing himself to rest for a bit and smoke.

The Marines that had come down from the hill were gaunt, and sleep-deprived. They were covered in a mixture of dirt and blood.

"Heard you guys had it bad last night. Anything you could tell us that might help us for tonight? Command just gave us orders to hold this position without much information on what to expect." Binks asked.

Obrian inhaled deeply on his cigarette and then blew out a very long and slow breath as he watched the cloud of smoke and vapor drift up. "Yeah. Probably won't be any vehicles, they came south through the trees, didn't use the roads, so there is no support train or tanks or armor that you need to worry about. Just a shit ton of Chinese infantry. Way it was yesterday was three waves in the attack, and from what I hear that seems to be standard for them." Obrian paused for a second and took another drag from his cigarette and a look of contemplation crossed his face. "Well" he continued "technically four waves, first was recon, kinda just pot shots here and there and they will probe the line to see what you have set up and where. The first real wave came strong and well-armed, fighting tooth and nail, the second wave was partially armed and the unarmed ones would pick up the guns from the dead first wave, the third wave was all their officers with burp guns killing anybody that tried to retreat and then attacking. So I would expect something like that tonight. They have grenades, at least some of them do and they use them in close, so look out for that…" The Marine paused here to think if there was anything else to mention while pulling hard and long on the cigarette in his mouth. "That's about it. There a fuckin million of em'…. Just dig in and fight and maybe you will be alive tomorrow." Obrian stated this last part with a slight smile and a glint in his eye.

Binks was silent as Obrian took a final drag on his cigarette then tossed it on the frozen ground and stood up amid a grunt of strain. The Marines helped their wounded comrade to his feet and continued their journey to the aid station. The general mood of Binks's squad had changed. They had all heard some gunfire while marching from Inchon and they had been aware that they would probably see some combat, but now it was starting to set in that it was going to happen soon and it would be a brutal fight.

His men were focused. They had a clear mission and fields of fire and knew they were about to be tested as men and Marines more than ever before. Reports were circulating about the sheer numbers that the Chinese were attacking with. There were multiple divisions of Chinese as opposed to the single Marine division that was spread out over several miles and consisted of a large number of support troops that were not considered to be combat troops.

Binks motioned for the team leaders and passed on what he had just been told. There was a sort of nervous energy among the men. Binks walked over to Smith and put his hand on his shoulder.

"It's gonna be a real fight…but we will hold this position until the last man." The words sounded calm and confident, but his mouth and throat felt dry and his stomach felt unsettled. He knew no matter what happened, he would not show his men how nervous he was.

"Of course," Smith answered while inspecting and cleaning his BAR. A moment of silence passed between the two and then Smith said "I'm here, in a war and I have never failed to do my duty in my life. I have never let my men down in combat, but until my last breath, I will always wonder if I have it in me to die well. To die fighting. To truly be a warrior at the moment that it will matter the most. It's odd, it's a test I would never want to have to face, but it's a test that I would like to know that I would pass if it came to that. I hope I make it," he paused for a moment and looked up at Binks "I hope WE make it, but a small part of me wants to pass that final exam of life." Smith thought for a few seconds then let out a snort "Sounds stupid when I say it out loud. Wish I could just shut my brain off till tomorrow, I always get the craziest thoughts and ideas the closer I get to a fight."

"It's normal." Binks said then putting a hand on Smiths' shoulder he stood up and said "You will do fine. Just focus on the mission." Then he walked to inspect the line one more time.

The Marines were shuttling back and forth between the line and the ammo depot and bringing with them as much ammunition as they could carry. The M20 rounds were heavy, each Marine could only handle at most two at a time one over each shoulder or one under each arm depending on how you wanted to carry it. There were some rounds that we're still in crates and one Marine on either side of them could move the crates about 20 to 30 yards at a time before having to stop set a down and readjust their grip.

Each round weighed just over 20lbs so five rounds were just over 100lbs. The Marines were malnourished from being on the road and more than a little bit exhausted from all the movement they had been doing the last couple of weeks since landing at Inchon, so they were a little more exhausted than normal when all the ammunition was finally assembled in the three fighting positions and ready to go.

Binks walked to each of the three fighting positions re-inspecting the fields of fire and making sure that all avenues of approach were appropriately covered. He checked to make sure that everybody knew about the proper communication systems and what to do in every event when the attack comes. Around 1600 there was nothing else they could do to prepare; the holes were done properly avenues of approach were covered and all the ammunition that they could get from the ammo depot was on site.

Binks personally walked around once again to the three fighting positions and checked with every one of his Marines asking them how they were doing and reassuring them that he was confident in their ability to fight and defend their positions at all cost. Once all this had been done all that was left to do was watch and wait. Binks sat down on the back end of the fighting hole that he had helped first team dig and stared down the valley towards where the enemy would most likely be approaching and envisioned them attacking while preparing himself for anything that might be happening later that night.

He began to formulate a plan in his head that would, if successful, hold the Chinese at bay no matter how many there were or how fast they came. Binks knew from what the Marines on their way to the aid station had told him, that there would be a recon element to feel out the lines and see what the defenses were like, so he began to think of a plan to lure them into a trap. He would defend the probing recon attack with rifles only. If Binks defended the attack with only riflemen, hopefully, the Chinese would think that is all they had defending this position. Then when the main attack comes, he could take them by surprise with the M20's and BAR's.

There were 13 Marines total in his section guarding this road, three had BARs, so 10 with rifles that could fire them, but when the recoilless rifles were operating, they took two Marines per, which left four rifles and three BARs and three M20's in the fight. The M20's could fire once every 15 seconds when they were moving fast, so with rotating the rounds from the first team to 2nd team and then to 3rd team, there would be one M20 round going downrange every five seconds.

They would open with rifles as far out as they could see them, but the M20's and BARs would stay silent until they began to funnel into the choke point, at which time first team BAR would open up while first-team M20 fired one round downrange followed immediately by 2nd team BAR and 2nd team M20 which would be followed immediately by 3rd team BAR and 3rd team M20. If done correctly, there should be almost no stopping in the automatic fire, since first-team BAR should have its gun reloaded by the time that 3rd is done dumping its magazine of rounds…and the time between M20 HE rounds should be close to five seconds of separation between them, which should be perfect since the casualty radius is about 30 yards which was roughly half the width of the choke point.

Each M20 would aim at a different part of the kill zone with the intent of killing everyone in it and leaving enough time to reload and kill anyone that would replace them in that zone. He sent a message to the company commander with a request for a radio operator so they could call for mortars as well. If they could add mortars to the defense, and time it correctly, it would be impossible for any Chinese to get through the valley. With his plan of defense completed, Binks sat there and reflected after a while about the fact that tonight might be his last night, as with any night or any moment that he was in Korea.

While he may not know which bullet had his name on it, if any of them did at all or whether or not he would survive this war and make it back to America, he would eventually one day die… and there was no way that anybody could ever know when exactly they were going to die unless you took your own life. So those people back in the United States, his friends, and his family were no more certain that they would not die today than he was of whether or not he would live through this war or even just this battle. Whether he would get hit by a bus when he went home to visit when this was all over or hit by a bullet tonight Binks was faced with his mortality. He never realized how much he loved to just sit and be alive more than when he was faced with the possibility of imminent death. The cold wind he had hated this last month felt like a familiar old friend, the snow looked more beautiful now than ever, and the moon seemed somehow alive. He felt connected to the universe.

He thought about a story one of his friends had told him when they were in basic training together. His friends' dad had bought his mother flowers on their anniversary and had stepped out into the street and gotten hit by a car…not a car that he didn't see, a car that he saw coming. The car was in the next lane so the Marines father had thought he was fine but the driver was drunk and not paying attention…the drunk driver had swerved over and hit his dad and a crumpled bleeding mass lay on the road where a loving man with flowers had stood a moment before. That was it. A life snuffed out. He collapsed into a sack of meat and bones spread across the asphalt just as the many Marines that Binks had seen collapsed on the road from Inchon. Another shit way to die, Binks thought to himself.

A warrior's death. Something that many men who die of old age and their deathbeds sometimes wish they could have had. There were certainly worse ways to go. But then what is the point of the warrior's death? Whom does it help? How does other people seeing my death as being honorable help me at all in the afterlife? Binks reflected on these things. What is death? My body is just a body and nothing more than meat and bones, no different from a cow. Maybe we are different because we have souls, but do we have souls? Binks had never seen a soul. He had ever touched a soul. He had ever smelled a soul. He had never heard of anyone proving that a soul existed. If there is a soul is it eternal? What happens to the soul after death? If there's a hell who goes to it? Because of this war do only the American troops go to heaven? Do only the Korean troops go to hell? Is it a mixture of all these things?

It must be, Binks thought. He had seen the Chinese prisoners, and they were forced to fight. They could be sound people that worship the deity, and as such the deity could not abandon them, so they must go to heaven as well. However, if men from both sides of this war are going to heaven, then why are we here? Who decides who goes? Who decides which army is on the right ethical side of this war? What are countries anyways but invisible lines drawn by others? Why should we fight and kill because some man in an office in Washington DC told us to? Why is doing that considered an honorable thing? How is it not a stupid thing, to blindly follow what others tell you to do? What happens when you die if you do have a soul?

On the off chance that there is a God and we do have souls, Binks thought he had better pray to him and let him know that he was thankful for the opportunity to have lived as long as he did, and that he would do his best to die well and that he hopes that the God will forgive him for any transgressions and allow him to forgo being tortured for all of eternity in hell, but instead allow him into heaven. Binks sent his prayer up to the heavens, not directed at any deity in particular but just to the cosmos at large, knowing that in his heart it was a pure message. He did not mean to offend whatever gods there were or whatever singular God. He was genuinely asking for forgiveness for anything he may have done in his lifetime to offend the gods or the singular deity.

If the God, or gods were forgiving, they would see that he was a good man and forgive him. Binks felt confident that any god that was fair would recognize that his heart was in the right place, and whether or not he called him by the right name, whether it be Allah, God, Abba; this fair God would allow Binks into heaven if he should die tonight. If Binks had such a thing as a soul, and if there was such a thing as heaven.

Having done this he felt confident that his spiritual mental and psychological well-being were as good as they were going to get and that his spirit was taken care of, he pulled out a cigarette while the sun was still up, and begin to smoke knowing that as soon as the sun started to set they would not be allowed to smoke since the light from the cigarettes would give away their position in the dark. As he pulled on the cigarette methodically and allowed his mind to drift, the last few rays of sunlight showed on his face as the sun dropped behind the mountains to the west. Once again he found a moment of comfort in focusing on the feelings the sunshine and the wind brought him. Binks closed his eyes and cleared his mind as he counted the breaths coming in and out of his body. When he got to 10 he put out his cigarette and then he visited the three teams fighting positions once again to check in on the men.

The time that passed after the sunset was filled with tension and anxiety among the Marines as they awaited their greatest test yet as warriors. The attacks initially started to their west on the positions of higher ground where the Chinese had hammered last night and were unsuccessful in taking and based on the way the sounds of gunfire drifted to him, Binks knew the fighting was intense.

They could hear the fighting about a little less than a mile away. The artillery behind them was firing over their heads and then the rounds of the artillery impacting in the distance lit up the sky for brief moments. They could hear the thump of mortars being dropped into and launched from their tubes followed by the sound of their rounds impacting, adding to the chaos. The Chinese attack was underway.

Sgt. Binks and his men sat in silence watching their fields of fire. Soon it would be their turn and they would be the ones taking part in the furious battle they could hear raging to the west. Right before 2300, they took contact.

Chapter 4

To the west, the illumination rounds kept the sky lit. They were launched from mortar tubes and popped high above the enemy where they began to burn brightly as they drifted towards the ground under a small parachute that slowed their descent. The incineration of the pyrotechnic candles cast a flickering light across the snow as they floated towards the earth. The cold air and flickering lights reminded Sgt Binks of a Christmas eve candlelight service that his parents made sure the whole family went to every year. It felt weird to be disconnected from the fighting and to observe it from afar. The beauty of the falling illumination rounds was accompanied by a feeling of emptiness at the recognition that under those lights' men were breathing their last breaths. Without the knowledge of what was happening, one might be forgiven for smiling at the flashing display and thinking of how it looked just like the 4th of July in the United States.

These observations took only a few seconds and then Binks brought his attention back to his section and the road they were tasked with defending. It was dark, but there was some visibility from the moon and its moonlight reflecting off the snow. They could see for about 100 yards pretty well, not as well as in daylight, but well enough to make out the road and to detect movement; that was what was most important to Binks.

It's a good position we have, he thought to himself. He glanced to his right and looked at the Marine next to him and saw his eyes, alert and scanning left to right and then right to left while he opened and closed his right hand to make sure it didn't go numb from the cold and function properly when he needed it to. The man Binks saw next to him was a true warrior and a cold and calculated killer. Sgt. Binks thought about how he was glad the men next to him were on his side because he would sure as hell hate to have to fight them. The sound of someone lumbering up from behind came to Binks' ears, and he recognized immediately the sound of clinking gear and rustling frozen trousers to be another Marine.

Binks looked back and saw that despite the horrendous amount of noise the Marine was generating he appeared to be attempting to approach quietly. The Marine paused as he tried to decide where in the defensive line he should be and Sgt. Binks saw by the light of the moon a dumbfounded look on his face. Binks waved his hand so that the approaching man could see. The awkward lump of clothing and gear labored through the last few steps of snow and knelt next to Sgt Binks.

"I'm looking for Sgt Binks." The Marine said quietly.

"That's me," Binks said and then waited for more information to come.

He noticed the Marine was young and had a radio on his back. Probably a battalion radio operator and the heavy radio was the reason he seemed to be moving with such abnormal difficulty.

"The battalion Ex-O sent me over here. Since this is one of the most likely avenues of approach, he wants me here to call in missions to the mortars." The out of breath Marine explained.

"Ok. Good. Hop in here." Binks motioned to the space to his left and indicated that the Marine should join him in the fighting hole while they waited.

The intensity of the attack to the west was picking up speed and the sound of chattering gunfire was drifting in at an ever-increasing rate. Binks once again looked down the path they were defending and started scanning right to left forward and then back left to right, probing into the night as far as his eyes would allow. His eyes fell on an odd shape in the snow about 150 meters away and he paused for a second to examine it. He shifted his rifle and aimed at the shape.

His eyes were straining into the darkness to decipher whether it was a mound of discolored snow or a person. He watched intently for any movement while keeping the sight of his rifle steady on the object. Binks moved his right thumb just slightly and the safety on the rifle clicked off, and even among the sound of gunfire and explosions in the distance, that sound seemed immeasurably louder than the rest. His heartbeat was picking up speed, and he drew a deep breath in and held it to calm his heart and steady his hand as his index finger began to slowly apply pressure to the trigger.

He was breathing slow and was laser-focused. All the explosions and gunfire faded into the sound of his heartbeat in his ears, he locked in on this one task. His mind was devoid of all the existential musings and observations of the absurdity of human nature that had been present a few moments before. The shape moved in an unmistakably human way and Sgt. Binks tensed his index finger slightly without moving any other part of his body. The muzzle flashed, the shape went limp and Binks yelled out "Contact front!!" As he yelled out, from seemingly nowhere, 50 Chinese were closing in as fast as they could run from the darkness 150 meters away. He found another target quickly and watched it collapse behind his muzzle flash.

The Chinese were now up and running towards the line, a few of them shooting, but mostly they were trying to close the distance. There were 14 Marines now in the line covering the road, including the radio operator, and Binks. Three had BAR's, 11 had rifles. All 11 rifles opened up as the Chinese started to close in. They were dropping quickly since they stood out in the full moonlight, and by the time they reached the 100m marker, there were only about 35 still trudging through the snow towards them. first Teams BAR opened up on the 100m mark and dusted off three Chinese with its first magazine and caused another 10 to dive for cover.

The automatic weapon had slowed them down a bit and there were only 25 left by the time they hit the 50m marker, and 2nd team BAR opened up as well and started to catch the Chinese in the crossfire of the two BAR's. The attack was now halted at about 40m away, a few were brave enough to keep rushing in, and they were immediately chopped down. The Chinese got up and retreated, no doubt to report on how the probe had gone. Of the 50 that attacked, only six made it off into the edge of the darkness and disappeared.

Binks motioned for the team leaders to come over and then passed the plan for the next attack. "Since they knew we had at least two BAR's and a squad of riflemen, the next time we make contact, open with both first and 2nd team BAR's right off the bat, 3rd team BAR you wait until they hit the 100m marker. At that time I want all the M20's firing in succession. First team, you start it off, then 2nd, then 3rd. Hopefully, we will have mortars dropping on the 100m mark as well, and we can catch them by surprise." He told the radio operator to call in for a fire mission on a target point 100m out when the Chinese were 150m out. The mortar rounds took time to travel through the air and that way the rounds would start impacting right when the Chinese would be crossing into the kill radius of the mortars.

Once again, the Marines were staring out over a motionless, silent, and cold Korean countryside. The wind had started to pick up, blowing snow in the faces of the Marines. Binks scanned as far as he could into the night, but the blowing snow made visibility about 50 meters less than before. Binks knew that the Chinese would try to take advantage of his lack of visibility. They will come again soon.

15 minutes passed and nothing happened. The fighting to the west had stopped. It was quiet, and still. Binks's eyes were constantly scanning, while his mind began to drift again. The bitter cold reminded him of winters in the United States. The way the cold bit into your skin and seemed to cut deep so that it felt as if your bones themselves were cold. Feeling the cold back home was always a sort of welcome pain because it usually meant that inside the house there was a crackling fire accompanied more often than not by some hot cocoa and a usual general sense of happiness in the evening especially when it was close to Christmas. Those had been good, clean, days. Fun and innocent days of a little rough and tumble fighting with brothers alongside good food made by mothers and aunts. It was Nov. the 19th today, so back home they would be getting ready for Thanksgiving to happen within the next couple of days.

He remembered one time when he was out on a cold day just like this, wearing just a sweater and shorts when one of the neighboring farmers drove by in an old rust bucket of a truck. The farmer had stopped in the middle of the road looked over at Binks in shorts and said "I always knew you was only half loaded boy." Laughing as he had driven away.

Life had been hard for that old farmer, and he had offered on a few occasions pieces of wisdom that Binks did not fully appreciate at the time. The same way life had been tough on the men to that were to the left and right of Sgt Binks in that ravine. It seemed to Binks like existence itself had been rough for everyone. If life is not nice, why make it worse? Why am I here in this country killing these men who probably want the same things, in the core of their being that I do?

Fuck it is cold.

Binks wanted to be next to a warm fire.

That's probably what the Chinese want right now as well, Binks thought to himself. Maybe that is why they seemed so intent on running into the lethal US Marine defensive line. Perhaps they just wanted to be out of the cold by any means, including death. Binks thought to himself as he kept his eyes on the horizon and methodically opened and closed his hands to keep the blood flowing. It was very quiet. Every small noise traveled far. Binks' stomach rumbled from hunger, the sound of which bothered Sgt. Binks more than the feeling of hunger.

Binks's eyelids were beginning to feel heavy. It was nearing midnight and he was starting to crash after the adrenaline rush of the earlier gunfight. The long days without rest, the sleepless nights, the malnutrition, and the cold had all gripped his consciousness and were pulling it towards a deep slumber.

He blinked very slowly, and his eyes seemed incapable of returning to a fully open position. They were stuck halfway up. He blinked again and they only rose one-quarter of the way back up. Then they snapped fully open.

Absolute silence lay over the land like an invisible blanket and the lack of noise offered the endless possibilities of what may arise from that void. No artillery, no flares, and no small arms fire. No potshots or explosions happening anywhere. Something wasn't right. It took a few seconds for his foggy and frozen brain to recognize what it was that made him perk up…he heard something in the distance. A faint noise he couldn't quite place. It sounded like wind blowing in distant trees. Noise traveled far in the quiet, and before he could even see them, he finally recognized it was the sound of hundreds of boots crunching in the snow.

"Standby for contact!" Binks yelled to bring the attention of the section to what was about to happen, then he turned to the radio operator and said:

"Give me illumination 300 meters out and have them get ready to start dropping H.E."

The RO started talking into the radio and Binks looked left and right to make sure that all the teams were up and ready. The Radio Operator started chattering into the radio to get the Mortars ready. The sound of rustling and the clicking of safeties, the double-checking of accessibility of ammunition, and then absolute silence again except for the faint sound in the distance of a horde running in the snow.

Behind him, Binks heard the deeper "thump" sound of mortars being dropped into tubes and he peered into the darkness through the sights on his rifle and waited to acquire a target as soon as the sky lit up. The first Illumination round popped, and a company of 300 Chinese was revealed, about 200 meters out. The entire line of rifles started firing. Binks aimed and started squeezing off rounds as quickly as he could line up targets.

First team BAR began opening fire and shooting their M20 into the front of the approaching company. 2nd teams M20 and BAR opened up followed by 3rd team and then right as 3rd teams BAR clicked on the empty magazine first was reloaded and opened up fire again. The radio operator was calling a 'fire for effect' mission about 100m forward of the line. The Chinese were still about 175m away and struggling uphill and in the snow as fast as they could. The sound of mortars from the battalion mortars stopped as they adjusted ranges and started switching from illumination rounds to high explosive rounds. The line kept firing at a frantic pace and between the three

M20's and BAR's, there was constant heavy fire going downrange.

The operator fed the command through the radio and Binks turned and continued to shoot at the approaching force. What followed was a perfectly timed bombardment on the approaching Chinese. Around 30 Chinese were already downed by the BARs, riflemen, and constant M20 rounds, leaving 270 attacking Chinese when they started crossing the impact area for the mortars. Each mortar team was dropping a HE rounds every five seconds, and with 10 mortar teams firing, there was a round impacting every half of a second.

The perfect combination wreaked havoc on the approaching Chinese. They continued to attack, but their numbers were cut in half by the mortars. Binks could see through the mortar bombardment that what was left of the attacking element was retreating. He motioned to the radio operator to cease fire on the mortars. The operator called it in, and the mortars and illumination stopped, and once again a dark silence drifted down from the black night sky, and the moon's emotionless face stared at Sgt Binks in a way that seemed rather smug to him.

The moon was there, but not a part of what was happening. It played a part because its illumination was reflecting off the white snow and helping men to kill other men, but it seemed unbothered by that. To

Binks, the moon appeared to be a rather condescending spectator.

Binks labored out of his fighting hole with some difficulty, impeded as he was by all the layers of clothing, and walked over to the other holes and checked to see about ammunition and casualties. A few nicks and scratches among some of the men from ricochets, but that was all. There was still a good supply of ammunition. He walked back to his hole and dropped in. Binks was able to pull a watch out of an inside coat pocket and make out in the light of the moon that it was just past midnight.

A gentle breeze blew in from the west and touched his cheeks, and he was struck by the thought that the same wind must have passed over the dead that lay from the battle that had taken place to the west earlier that day. Once again, the cold dug its icy teeth into Sgt. Binks' bones. He pulled tobacco leaves out and stuffed them between his left cheek and molars while he folded his arms and began scanning again. A gust of wind blew, and he squinted his eyes as they began to moisten from the frigid air. Blinking a few times to clear his vision after the wind died down, he took another peek at his watch and saw that it was nearing about half an hour after midnight. The Marines earlier had said to expect three attacks, so there would probably be another attack coming.

Binks heard the sound of what seemed like a slight thump of two solid objects connecting with force, but not speed. He looked over and saw that one of the Marines had fallen asleep standing up and his helmet had saved him from having his forehead smash into the front sight on his rifle when his head had collapsed forward. Binks told the teams to go down to half-watch then he returned to his position and waited.

Chapter 5

A painfully cold and eerily quiet hour passed so slowly it felt like 10 hours. Binks looked down again at his watch. His eyes took a second to focus before he was able to tell that it was half-past one in the morning, and then he struggled to bring his head upright again.

He thought of a time when he and Smith had been talking on the long walk here. Smith had asked Binks how he would want to die in this war if he could choose. "Surrounded by dead enemies." Had been Sgt. Binks' response.

Smith looked at him, "That's the only good way there is."

A cloud had drifted in between him and the moon, killing the small amount of illumination the moon had previously offered. The night was now as black as tar. He looked up at the moon and saw the edge start to appear as the cloud drifted farther North and slowly started to illuminate the night again. He heard a sharp movement to his left and he turned to look towards the unmistakable sound of a safety clicking off cutting through the silent air. It took a second for him to focus, but he saw one of the Marines looking intently down his rifle and as soon as that image registered in his brain, the muzzle flashed.

That shot in the night seemed more deafening than any other sound Sgt. Binks had ever heard. The sound snapped him back to reality and he looked in the direction the shot had gone. He was fully awake now and saw that there was another attack coming up the slope. This one was about the same size as the last, 300 strong. They had been slower and more methodical in this last approach, using the cover of the cloud, and had managed to get within about 150 meters before they had been spotted. The entire line now erupted in firing towards the oncoming Chinese.

Binks quickly turned to the radio operator. "Give me illumination and an HE 'fire for effect' right now!" Binks yelled.

His heart rate had shot through the roof and his mouth immediately felt dry. He had been snapped back to war when he had been on the verge of falling asleep and his body had responded by dumping adrenaline into his system. As he began to fire on the approaching Chinese, he knew the mortars would not impact fast enough to make a difference this time and the horde of enemy soldiers would be on top of their one squad defensive line in less than 45 seconds.

He turned back to the operator, pulled him closer, and said in a much dryer voice loud enough only for him to hear, "Tell Battalion they will take us out, and they will take the position if we don't get reinforcements right fucking now." The operator talked into the radio and Binks returned to firing.

They were about 140m out and closing. Silhouettes were moving in the distance that looked surprisingly similar to the targets they had practiced on before the deployment. They lacked the distinguishing features that make them individuals. He took aim at one of the silhouettes, squeezed off a round, and watched as it collapsed.

130m and closing. He dropped another.

120m and closing. The shape he was aiming at disappeared into an explosion from 3rd teams' m20. He shifted and shot at another but missed. Realizing he was no good to anyone if he didn't calm down, he took a deep breath and seeing the remaining 280 men thought *I fight until I die* and took aim once again.

110m and closing. He dropped another.

100m. Deep breath and another shape hit the ground.

90m. Again.

80m. Again.

70m. The radio operator was mid-sentence when the sound of metal hitting metal at a high speed was followed by his body going limp and collapsing behind Binks. The now-dead radio operator's body hit the back of Sgt. Binks' knee and caused it to buckle as he pulled the trigger.

'*Fuck*' Sgt. Binks thought, '*a life snuffed out and a wasted shot.*'

60m. Binks could see the individual parts of the bodies. They were no longer just shapes. He dropped another body.

50m. The mortar rounds started landing. Too late. Nearly all the Chinese were on the close side of the kill zone. The illumination rounds popped overhead right as he pulled the trigger.

40m. The fire mission was in full force and mortar rounds were exploding at about two per second. The Chinese were unaffected as all the rounds were impacting *behind* the attacking company. Binks' rifle ran out of ammunition and he quickly grabbed the dead radio operator's rifle and returned to firing as fast as he could aim it.

30m. They had faces. One face disappeared behind his muzzle flash.

20m. The faces had mouths, and noses and the bullets they fired were missing by a much smaller margin. There were still at least 200 Chinese and Binks knew they would be on top of him and his men in five seconds. He also knew the Chinese outnumbered them more than 15 to 1.

Binks shot at one of the charging men, and the soldier's head snapped back and touched his shoulder blades before he collapsed on the snow. He aimed at the next closest Chinese soldier, but he dropped before Binks pulled the trigger. A heavy volley of firing came to Binks' ears from behind him, and it began to cut through the Chinese in front of him.

Golf company and Charlie company had been sent as reinforcements and they began to beat back the assault. A grenade landed in the 3rd teams fighting hole and one of the Marines grabbed it to throw it out and it exploded in his hands. Third team's position went silent. Binks saw this and started making his way towards them to see if anyone was alive and if so, to pull them to safety.

A Chinese man grabbed the M20 from 3rd teams' position and began to run off with it. Binks quickly knelt and shot him in the back of the head. He then continued towards the 3rd teams' fighting hole and saw that the Chinese were retreating due to the defensive fire from Golf and Charlie Company.

As Sgt. Binks approached 3rd teams' fighting hole he slung his rifle and began to try to help the wounded Marines by attending to their wounds. Binks began to apply pressure to a shrapnel wound that was bleeding badly and the gunfire slowly subsided as the Chinese disappeared into the night. The blood was seeping out and over the top of his gloved hand as he said a few calming words to the injured man. He looked up in the direction that the Chinese had just disappeared into the night, searching for any movement, and noticed the M20 was no longer lying in the snow next to the Chinese soldier who had tried to take it.

Another Chinese soldier must have picked it up during the retreat.

Two companies that had been in regimental reserve had been sent after the last attack to fortify the position held by Binks and his men, they were on their way and nearly there when the attack had started. *If they would have been any farther away, we would have all been killed* Binks thought to himself as he helped load the wounded Marine on a stretcher to be carried back to the regimental medical aid station.

The feeling of nervous anticipation and fear was now replaced with one of confidence within the defensive line. The third attack having been repelled, Binks knew the Chinese were pulling back for the night to regroup. The Marines had begun to set up a watch rotation and lay out their sleeping bags as the realization that the fighting for the night was done, began to sink in. Low chatter and a few chuckles were heard as they began to try to find humor again as the adrenaline was replaced with relief to be alive. Binks looked around him and observed the strewn corpses that had previously housed lives, dreams, and personalities. The icy wind blew into their open eyes and dried out any sparkle that may have once been.

Four men from his section and the one battalion radio operator were killed in action. A quick count of the weapons and equipment showed that everything was accounted for except for the one M20. In addition to the five KIA, six had to be taken to the medical tent with minor wounds, making for a total casualty rate of 11 out of 14. Binks, Smith, and Jones were the only ones of the original defense left on the line. Binks again stared out at the expanse before him, where hours before had only been snow, lay hundreds of human-shaped lumps marked in contrast to the snow by their blood.

Fast-paced footsteps approached from behind him and the sound reached Binks' ears, but his eyes remained fixed on the sight before him.

"Looking for Golf company commander." A voice said, "Right here." another voice answered.

"Orders from regiment, everybody is pulling out, we are heading back. Going to Hungnam for evacuation. We are to break down this position immediately and move back a few miles tonight." The first voice said.

That message was immediately followed by a buzz and a small commotion as tired men began packing up sleeping bags and gear. Binks hopped up and quickly jogged over to first teams' hole where Smith and Jones were. He peeled off his outer jacket, stuffed it into his pack, and strapped his helmet to the top.

Kneeling next to smith he said "Take my pack. Put it on a truck and keep an eye on it. If anyone asks where I am say you haven't seen me since the attack." Then he stood back up and walked back to 3rd teams' hole where the missing M20 had been taken from after the grenade had gone off.

The Marines finished stuffing their packs for the march back towards regiment and staff NCOs urged them to move faster with the loving terms of endearment so common to the Marine vernacular.

"Hurry the fuck up."

Binks looked at the tracks in the snow next to the fighting hole and rather easily identified the tracks heading away from the hole towards the Chinese retreat. He slung his rifle over his shoulder and by the light of the moon, he began the hunt.

Chapter 6

Sgt. Binks' face was numb. Every few steps a thin mucus dripped from his nose into the snow, but he couldn't feel it. His feet were holding a fast rhythm while he kept the same short stride as the man whose tracks he followed. The tracks led him to a dead man about 100 meters from the fighting hole. There lay the soldier who he had killed for taking the M20. He examined the tracks leading away from the dead man. As confusing as they were, one set of tracks was deeper than the others. The weight of the M20 would explain the increase in depth for these tracks. He looked up to examine the direction they were going, then locked his eyes on the footprints and began a slow methodical jog in their trace.

The weight of the rifle on his shoulder and the feel of the sling threaded between his thumb and index finger was something he was quite accustomed to. The crunching of snow under his boots, the brittle fabric rubbing with each stride, and his ragged breathing combined to make an unmistakable assembly of sounds that Binks was very familiar with. Many times, as a kid he had hunted in the snow. Now he did so again, this time in pursuit of a more deadly prey.

This was who he was. He was never more alive than when stalking. He was never more alert than when hunting. Something primal within him was activated in those moments that was deeper than simple biology. At the very core of his soul this was what he was meant to do.

Like the opening of an arctic western shootout, the wind picked up and blew snow across the tracks he followed. It reminded him of a time when he had been hunting in the snow back home. The wind had been whipping snow into his eyes the whole hunt, as they were stalking a deer. They had come to the top of a small hill and found a buck attempting to breed with a doe. Binks had decided not to end the buck's life until it had the opportunity to create a new one. Despite the buck's attempts, the doe was not interested. She began to make her way towards the backside of the hill and out of Binks' line of sight. Binks didn't want to have to track the buck again if it disappeared into the woods, so he let out a slow breath and shot it in the heart as it was mid-leap following the doe. He remembered feeling connected to that buck.

Life seemed simple to Binks when he was observing wildlife. Wildlife seemed to perform the same basic things that humans did, but on much simpler terms. It seemed to Binks that the cognitive ability of humans to think, in many ways just caused more emotional pain. Animals did not wage war, or at least not in the way humans did. Humans were innovative killers with more than just a streak of evil. Humans had malice.

He allowed his mind to imagine briefly what a war would look like among animals. Thousands of Grizzlies from the Rocky Mountains against thousands from the Sierra Nevada Mountains, meeting to fight to the death in the middle of the two mountain ranges. The war would have started because the Rocky Mountain Grizzlies picked berries and stashed them as a group while the Sierra Nevada Grizzlies all picked and stockpiled as individuals.

Binks was brought back from this amusing train of thought by the need to readjust his rifle that had begun to slip off his shoulder. About another 100 meters in, the tracks stopped and it became clear that the soldier he was tracking had enlisted the help of another man to carry the burden. The two sets of tracks were cut deep and were easy to follow. He pulled a flask out from inside his left breast pocket and took a sip. He had kept it there as added protection since it sat right in front of his heart and was filled with water.

He had heard a story years ago in boot camp of a man who always kept a pocket-sized bible in his breast pocket, and it had saved his life when he had been shot. He figured a metal flask would be just as well for the same purpose. If a little leaflet of papers could save your life, a metal flask could probably do so as well. It also had very practical utility, as in this case, when all he wanted was just a tiny sip of water.

He took another sip and slid the flask back and buttoned the pocket so that it was secured in place. The flask was positioned in a way that prevented the pocket from buttoning, so he reached his hand in and repositioned it. He felt a rough part on the side of the otherwise smooth flask, where there were a few letters that had been engraved. It had been a gift from the girl back home. The inscription read, *Be Strong and of Good Courage.*

He was nearing the top of a small hill and he slowed his pace down to a quiet walk, staying in the footsteps of his prey, to minimize the sound of crunching snow. As he approached the crest of the hill, he dropped to a crouch and unslung his rifle. The top of the hill was clear so he moved behind a boulder and looked to find anything that his eyes might pick up.

A cloud moved over the moon and he reached into his pocket for another sip of water while he waited for the cloud to pass. As the last bit of the cloud continued on its' way in life, and the landscape before him was again illuminated by the ever-watchful moon, he saw them. A group of six Chinese soldiers, two of which were clearly struggling under a burden and walking slowly. The other four were there to assist when needed, it appeared.

They had fallen a few hundred meters behind the main element which was starting its ascent over the next hill across from the small valley he now looked over. Binks slung his rifle and descended the same way he had come, running faster now than before. Sunlight would be only a few hours away, and he would stand no chance when it was fully light outside.

He reached the base of the hill and then ran as fast as he could around it until he was at their tracks again, but without having exposed himself on the open face of the hill like he would have if he had followed the tracks directly. He could see where they were headed by looking at the 90 or so Chinese in the main element that was now several hundred yards ahead. He darted from mound to mound to keep his concealment as he quickly closed the gap between him and his prey. Binks was gaining on them and was now within 350 meters. He wanted to get as close as possible without being noticed.

He saw a small dip in the snow that seemed to follow some natural terrain underneath that veered off to the left and he quickly made his way to it and began to run along with the natural concealment. His breathing was heavy, and the cold air seemed to burn his throat and lungs with every breath. His throat was dry and he was on the verge of vomiting from exertion. His face was now completely numb, mucus was flowing from his nose, his eyes watering at the corners continuously from the dry cold wind. His legs and hands were now numb as well.

The drift he was following began to rise and flatten out, and he slowed down and quietly walked to the top of the embankment. He paid attention to his nose as he drew a deep breath attempting to recognize any smells. He could faintly hear some sort of noise in the distance that he could not quite make out. His eyes were constantly shifting, looking to take in every possible identifiable detail of his surroundings.

The sound became less vague and he could hear voices. He was very close. He crouched lower and slowly stepped forward hardly making a sound at all. His eyes broke the plane and he could see them. The last of the lead element had disappeared over the hill ahead, and the group of six were about to start the climb. Binks unslung his rifle and clicked the safety off.

They were about 60 meters away. Binks didn't want to risk missing if he aimed for their heads with only the dim light of the moon. Aiming at the center of the Chinese soldier closest to him, he slowly began to exhale as he squeezed his index finger against the trigger.

Chapter 7

Binks could feel his heart pounding from the exertion of the run while he slowly applied pressure to the trigger. The rifle bucked, the muzzle flashed, and he immediately switched targets. The Chinese stopped walking and had barely even registered that they had heard a shot when he pulled the trigger the second time. There were six targets in total. Two of them were on the ground, two were still holding the M20, and the other two turned to try and see where the shots were coming from while unslinging their rifles. They were bunched together, these last four, and he moved quickly.

With speed, he went left to right and fired into the center of each one before they had a chance to identify where the attack was coming from. After sending one round into each standing chest, two collapsed immediately, two stayed standing. He used his last two rounds on them and before they had even started to fall to the snow, he had slung his rifle across his back, drew his pistol, and began running as fast as he possibly could towards them. It had taken less than four seconds.

He knew that the shots would cause the lead element to turn around to investigate. He had only seconds before rounds started coming his way. He covered 50 meters in about 10 seconds. His legs were burning from the exertion of running in unpacked snow and his lungs felt as though they were about to explode as he sucked in the sub-freezing air.

He stopped 10 meters away. Aiming at the base of the neck he quickly put two more rounds into each of the bodies. If he shot high it would hit the neck, low would hit the lungs, and left or right would at least break a collarbone on the off chance any of them were just playing dead. He ran over to the M20 that now lay on the contorted body of one of the men who had been carrying it. Kneeling, he quickly grabbed the breech lock in the back of the tube and removed it from the rest of the recoilless rifle, rendering it useless.

He tucked the breech lock under his left arm and then quickly reloaded his pistol and rifle as he started to walk back in the direction he had come from. With the breech lock tucked under his left arm, it was difficult to reload, but he did it as quickly as possible. Rounds started impacting the snow a few feet away from him. He immediately finished loading and broke into a run retracing his steps back towards the friendly lines as the sounds of the gunshots finally caught up with him.

A few more shots went off, none of them close enough for Binks to even notice where they were impacting. A few more seconds and he was out of the line of sight of the Chinese. He ran as hard as he possibly could to put some distance between himself and the main element of the Chinese, and only began to slow down when he began to dry heave. Binks felt annoyance with his bodies physical capabilities as he felt his mind was sharp and his body was reaching its limits.

He was holding the breech lock in his left hand as he ran, with his rifle sling in his right hand. He had lost all feeling in his fingers and the lock slipped out and sunk about a foot into the snow. He was freezing, and it took a couple of seconds before he noticed it wasn't in his hand anymore. He immediately pivoted back and picked it up. He glanced back to see if anyone was following and saw no indication of pursuit.

This time he held the breech lock pinched between his left forearm and left hip as he ran since his left hand would not close more than halfway. His right arm cradled his rifle. No longer did the sound of gunfire ring in the distance. Once again, silence and the sound of his boots in the snow as he tried to get back to his men as quickly as his body would allow. The sound of his ragged breathing reached his numb and sleep-deprived ears as if it was coming to him from underwater. Everything seemed to be moving slowly. His body, his mind, and time itself seemed to be moving at a snail's pace. The first hint of sunlight was starting to turn the eastern sky into a lighter shade.

It was still dark, but the stars were fading and the sky was a navy blue, where it had been black during the violence of the hours past. He was looking to the east, towards where he knew the sun would rise in about an hour, as he ran. Vaguely, through the mental fog, he noticed that something was off. He stopped dead in his tracks, and then, took a knee as he tried to figure out what it was that had triggered an alarm in his head. It took a few seconds before he realized what had alarmed him. There was a sound coming towards him. The sound of multiple boots crunching the snow beneath their rubber soles.

He unslung his rifle and clumsily clicked the safety off with his now barely functioning hand. Sgt. Binks could hear them approaching, but could not see them. They were about to crest a small snowdrift in front of him and Binks was fully exposed, with no time to run out of sight.

He was having trouble bringing the rifle to bear because of his now completely numb left arm. He put the stock under his right armpit, with his elbow pinching it into place, and the muzzle pointed in the direction of the potential threat. He shifted his hips back and brought his left knee into his chest. This allowed him to be a smaller target and offered the added protection of his shin bone against a bullet that would otherwise hit his heart. He saw the heads pop over the top of the drift, then the shoulders. They were looking at the ground, not expecting to run into any trouble since they had already left the front line. Sgt. Binks waited for them to walk towards him. He wanted them to expose themselves a little more.

There were three of them. Three Chinese soldiers. The one in the middle was injured and the other two were helping him walk by supporting his weight with their shoulders. Binks held his rifle as steady as possible and waited until they were about 15 meters away, then he started shooting. His first shot hit the one on the left in the chest, and he collapsed. As he fell, the man he was supporting fell with him.

The Chinese soldier on the far right dropped to his knees as he frantically began reaching for his gun. The gun had been slung behind his back and was now caught on a piece of his clothing. Binks squeezed off a few more rounds but his rounds, were missing and he couldn't force his body to cooperate and aim properly.

Binks tried to pull his pistol out of its holster but his fingers wouldn't move well enough. He didn't have time to reload so he stumbled to his feet and ran towards them as fast as he could. The wounded man began crawling towards the man who had been shot in an attempt to grab his gun. The soldier on the right had his weapon caught on his belt and was fumbling to dislodge it with hands that were undoubtedly like blocks of ice and refused to cooperate. The soldier on the right got his gun up in time to get off one round as Sgt. Binks ran towards him.

The round cracked very close to his head as he ran towards the Chinese. Binks grabbed the breech lock with his right hand from where it had been tucked under his left arm and swung it at the soldier on the right. The solid metal breech smashed into the Chinese soldier's temple. His head collapsed in and blood and brains oozed out. Like cracking an egg with red albumen and yolk. The soldier collapsed forward into the snow and Binks fell, off balanced from swinging the breech lock. The breech had slipped out of his hands and fallen a few feet away.

He paused and drew a few deep and ragged breaths of air in. Then, he heard a rustling noise and looked to see the wounded Chinese soldier that had been carried by the other two was crawling hand over hand towards his comrades' rifle on the ground a few feet away. Binks grabbed the breech lock and scrambled to where the wounded soldier was just about to grab his fallen soldiers' gun.

Binks went to swing and the man kicked at his knee at the same time, off-balancing him temporarily. The breech lock missed the soldier's head and hit his collarbone instead, which caved in under the blow. Part of the collarbone poked up out of the skin and the man let out a shriek. Binks swung the breech lock at his head for the second time. Once again, the man kicked and Binks lost his balance and fell beside the soldier who then grabbed a knife attached to his belt.

The man's right arm was immobile because of his shattered collarbone, but he began driving the knife towards Binks with his left arm. He did so with a force that showed despite being in his incapacitated state, he had no intention of dying without taking Binks with him. Binks clamped down on the man's arm, over-hooking with his left, around the wrist and then dropping his knee into the elbow. The soldier was strong, and his arm didn't break initially. Binks readjusted his weight and tried again and this time the elbow cracked. Then, Binks let the arm come forward a bit before yanking back again, the same way he would break a wet tree branch.

The soldier was still gripping the knife tightly, and Binks slowly twisted it out of his hands. The soldier was trying his hardest to move with two incapacitated arms and only one good leg. Binks dropped his left knee onto the soldier's rib cage with all his weight behind it, while posting out with his right leg for balance. His left hand cupped the back of the soldier's head and he held it steady. The soldier writhed underneath in a frantic attempt to escape, to no avail. His eyes were darting in every direction looking around desperately for help while he screamed in agony and despair.

Binks drove the knife into his neck just below the ear. The Chinese soldiers' eyes went wide and they locked with Binks'. The soldier screamed. The scream sounded as though he was gargling water as his blood seeped into his larynx. Binks could tell, based on the way the blood was pouring out, he had only nicked the carotid artery. Binks maintained eye contact with the soldier while he twisted the knife and completely severed the artery he had only partially cut. The arterial spray shot up and covered his whole face and he closed his eyes for a second, and when his eyes opened, they emerged from under a mask of red.

The screaming stopped. The absolute silence around him stood in stark contrast to the gunfire and desperate shrieking that had been there a few moments before. After the initial spray, the fountain of red had lost some of its force and was now just flowing out. Like a gentle pulsing spring of scarlet, it flowed over his hand and between his fingers like water over river rocks. Binks watched the blood gush from the Chinese soldier's neck, until it become a slow trickle revealing the knife and the hand that held it.

Binks would recognize that hand anywhere. It was a familiar hand. The large fingers and the lines in the knuckles were the same. Binks recognized the scarlet stained hand, and for a second he was a kid again staring at the hands of his father. He remembered what he had seen those hands do. They had built and fixed things with tools. Now it held a different tool, one to open a hole in the side of a human's neck and drain the blood out of him. Of all the things a man could do with his hands, it seemed a tragedy to use them like this. Binks felt like he was an outside observer of what had just happened.

He shook his head to clear it of the thought and clumsily stood to his feet. His breathing was still ragged from the exertion of the fight and his arms and legs felt heavy. Tucking the breech lock under his left arm he slung his rifle and again began to head South.

As the sun began to show above the tops of the hills to the east, Smith was walking up to the Commanding Officer to give his report of the Missing In Action, Killed In Action, and missing equipment from the attack the night before. Smith explained to the Captain that he and one other were the only ones not wounded from the section. There were six KIA, four WIA, and one MIA. The MIA was Sgt. Binks. The Captain acknowledged the report and slapped Smiths' shoulder. "You guys did a hell of a good job."

Before anything more could be said something caught Smith's attention coming down the embankment on the side of the hill. A solitary Marine moving towards them. The man was covered in dirt and blood. He appeared to be on the verge of collapsing from fatigue. He was walking like his left leg was bothering him a little, and he held something tucked under his left arm. He looked like a man who had been through hell. His eyes held a stare so cold and emotionless that it seemed to make the Korean winter feel warm in comparison. It was Sgt. Binks.

"The breech lock from the stolen M20, sir." Binks handed it to the CO.

The Captain stared, speechless for a moment, and then managed to muster a, "Thank you, Sgt."

There was silence all around as people stared at Binks, curious about where this blood-covered man had just come from.

Binks looked around and then glanced at Smith before asking, "Cigarette?"

Smith looked confused for a second, then realizing he had been asked a question, he muttered his recognition and reached to where he kept the cigarettes on the inside pocket of his outer coat. He found the pack and quickly withdrew one and began to raise it to offer it to Sgt. Binks. He paused halfway up and looked at Binks. Smith thought briefly of asking for details on what had happened, but thought that it was best to do so when not in the presence of the CO, and proceeded to hand Binks the requested cigarette.

The CO put his hand on Binks' shoulder and thought briefly about what to say. He felt love for this man who had gone through hell to retrieve the breech, so that the Chinese would not be able to make use of the stolen M20. He was a great leader, and a fearless warrior.

He could only imagine the difficulty that Binks must have endured to retrieve the breech lock. At that moment all the CO could think to say seemed insufficient to express what he felt in his heart. He looked into Binks' detached eyes and felt an immense amount of gratitude that this man was fighting on his side of the war. He nodded his head in silent acknowledgment of the man before him, a man that was covered with the now-dry and flaking blood of the night's conquest. He then turned and walked back to his jeep with the breech lock in hand.

Chapter 8

Binks stared out over the tall dry grass in front of him as he thought back to the fighting holes of Korea, and the internal philosophical battles the two sides of his brain took part in there. He wondered if he ever would have thought of life in the manner that he did if he had not faced death. If he had never gone to war; would he ever have paused to contemplate life in the way that he did? How many great philosophers that we will never know of were killed in wars?

The memories of the frozen hell in Korea were now a part of him. Binks felt that there are foundational memories that form the bedrock of who we are as humans, to make those memories with people that we care about is what really matters. Binks thought about his wife and his marriage. He remembered the wedding but his favorite memories of her came from when he was in Korea, knowing those moments might be his last. Thoughts of her had given him comfort in his greatest time of need.

In many ways when he held her now, he was holding himself in past. When he held her, he existed in a plane in which he was himself at that moment, while simultaneously being himself in a foxhole in Korea, and he was himself in the future knowing he would one day look back on these very moments for comfort someday. He wished he could go back to the scared man in the foxhole that he had been and hug him while telling him about what great emotional heights lay ahead for him when he finally made it home.

When he was in Korea the knowledge that someone cared enough to think of him helped him to have something to look forward to when he came home. It gave him something to want to return to. There was a part of him that loved being in a war zone, and while he hated that part of himself, it was something he had come to accept. He was well adapted to the darkness and evil of war and the thought of her waiting for him may have been the only thing that kept him from being swallowed completely by that abyss.

Thirteen long years had passed since that night in Korea and Binks was 42 now. The last thirteen years he had spent training Marines in Camp Pendleton. There was a new theatre of war that the United States was involved in now. Not a war, but a "conflict" in Vietnam. He had been preparing the next generation of Marines for Vietnam in training. Since the life cycle of most Marines were about four years (voluntarily or otherwise) he had trained the last three generations of Marines.

He had earned a Silver Star for his actions on that night in Korea. The medal's citation only mentions the defense of his position on the road that night. There was no official mention of Binks' run into and out of the enemy territory, since it never officially happened. Today was the last day of leave before going back for his final deployment. He was set to retire.

He was a Chief Warrant Officer in Explosive Ordinance Disposal now. No longer in the infantry technically, although he would be attached to a Special Operations Command unit when he got to Vietnam, or at least that was what he was told. Binks was sitting on his front porch in a rocking chair.

A warm breeze swept in from across the open land that lay before him. The wind blew and would blow whether or not he was here in this moment to experience the breeze. Like all things in nature, it just existed. The wind in a hurricane could kill a man, but you cannot hate the wind for having done it. It would have blown a gale just the same over those waters if there was no ship there. The wind could kill, but the wind was not violent. It held no ill will towards those it crushed with its' power. Men, on the other hand, do most things with either good or bad intent.

The wind had been with him in Korea, as it was with him now. When he was in Korea and he felt the wind he had thought how odd it was that the wind felt the same in war as it did in peace. Now, he thought about how the wind felt the same in peace as it did in the war. Every gust of wind was a reminder to Binks of the indifference the wind held towards the brevity and ruthlessness of human life.

His eyes were glazed over and he was staring at nothing in particular as he relived what it was like to feel a knife cut through another man's neck. A distant sound drifted to his ears. He furrowed his brow as he tried to identify what the noise was. It came to him again...*what is that?*

"Uncle?" A little voice said, repeating the attention-grabbing question for the third time, although it was the first time Binks had heard it.

Binks came back to reality in his Kentucky home and saw his brother's young son standing a few feet away from him and realized he had been talking to the boy before he had slipped off into his thoughts.

"Yes?" Binks answered.

"I asked you what war was like, Uncle." The boy said, apparently repeating a question that Binks had no memory of hearing.

"Oh," he said, now vaguely recalling that they had been engaged in a conversation a few seconds before. "It wasn't all that you might expect-" he paused and thought for a few seconds. "There was a whole lot of walking, and it was very cold. Very cold."

The boy's mother called for him and the boy said that he must go, but he wanted to hear more about the guns and airplanes in war after dinner. Then he was gone, and Binks again stared off over the open land. A few moments passed, then the sound of footsteps on the porch came to his ears.

He listened to the graceful gait. There was beauty even in just the sound of his wife's stride. He turned his head and looked at her as she walked across the porch, a book held between her hands. His heart could not stop from swelling, nor his lips from turning into a smile at the sight of her. She said hello and kissed his forehead and then, sat in the chair to his right.

She began to read her book, and he continued to admire her. How he had landed such a woman was beyond him. She possessed rare qualities in abundance. She was an angel sent just for him. She was intelligent and elegant and as calming and beautiful as a gently flowing brook. Her dark brown eyes had a deepness and sparkle that hinted at both her depth of character and lighthearted humor. A beautiful and rare gem of a woman, she was his greatest treasure.

He was no longer staring out over the open land in front of him with an empty and meaningless gaze. He was staring at her. She turned the page in her book. He watched her eyes move back and forth across the page as she read. The smile had not left his lips since he had first seen her walking across the porch. That was his whole world, right there.

A mosquito buzzed by his face, and he took a lazy swing at it with the flick of his wrist. His brother and his brother's wife were inside the house preparing dinner. They had come over to visit and said that

Binks and his wife should relax and spend time together while they cooked since this was Binks' last day home. The sun began to dip over the horizon as they sat together in silence. The mooing of a cow nearly exactly coincided with a call from his brother that dinner was ready. Binks and his wife walked inside and sat down at the dinner table.

His brother commented on how he didn't see the reason for all these U.S. troops going over to some foreign country that didn't ask for help to dip their fingers in something that they should not be dipping into. The way that Binks' brother saw things was that we should live and let live. Put the U.S. first in all things and forget about the other countries and their petty squabbles. Binks' brother looked over at him to see if his social and political views would be validated and Binks simply let out a thoughtful "Hmm," as he thought about the statement for a few seconds.

"Ours is not to question why, ours is but to do or die," Binks said, quoting a mutation of the poem by Lord Tennyson. "There are people that we have elected, who look at the big picture of things. They look at what is best for the future of the United States and they look at what the options are. We elected those people. If you don't have faith in them, you don't have faith in the people. I do. I have faith in the system, in the people of the United States, and by extension, the elected officials of the United States. When an elected official tells me to go somewhere and do a job that I am very good at, I have faith that he has made the right decision."

His brother nodded his approval and the conversation shifted to the plans that Binks and his wife had for after the deployment. He was looking forward to the retirement that awaited him. They would build a small cabin near Flathead Lake in Montana and spend the rest of their lives living off the land and the pension from his coming military retirement.

He had a vision of what life would be like. The clear Montana skies in the summer and the beautiful Flathead Lake would make for perfect fishing and relaxing in the evening. Fresh snowfall in the winter would cover all the imperfections in the world in a pure white coating and they would stay close to the fire to stay warm. The geographic location of the vision was not nearly as important as the fact that every future he could envision was one in which he was side by side with his wife.

At the dinner table, his nephew Nick was having a little trouble chewing some of the meat that had been served. The toughness of the meat was proportional to the toughness of the deer that Binks had harvested from two days prior during a hunt. Nick was tearing at the meat on his fork with his not yet fully developed teeth when the mother got up and retrieved a steak knife from the kitchen to cut the boy's meat into smaller pieces for him. Binks watched the knife slice through the meat and again his mind went back to that day in Korea when he had cut into the neck of that Chinese soldier. To the other observers, they saw a steak knife cutting deer meat, but in Binks' eyes, there was blood spurting out of the meat, the way it had out of the soldier's neck. His heart beat faster, and his stomach began to tighten. His sister-in-law finished the task of cutting the meat and put the knife away, and Binks' heart, stomach, and mind relaxed.

Binks smiled at the boy at said, "What a thoughtful mother you have, eh?"

The boy nodded and uttered a sound that was an attempt at saying thanks around the food in his mouth.

To those around him, Binks had looked normal throughout. There was no indication of the internal turmoil he had just felt or the temporary increase of adrenaline at the vision he had. Binks looked over and made eye contact with his wife and smiled. Her eyes calmed his mind and the evening carried on.

After dinner, he headed outside as the sun was beginning to set and began to toss a baseball back and forth with his nephew. The conversation was idle talk about what was going on in the news and what was on the boy's mind. Binks asked him if he had developed any thoughts on girls yet. The boy said that he didn't interact with them much, but he supposed he would one day, although it didn't matter much either way to him at the moment. Binks smiled as he seemed to remember feeling that exact way when he was the boy's age. The first time a girl had ever told him she liked him, he had been surprised. He had never thought of himself as being something that would be sought after or "liked". As a boy, he had liked throwing a baseball or swinging a stick while pretending it was a sword. To him, the word 'liked' seemed incredibly special as a kid. It made him blush.

Binks continued to throw the ball back and forth with his nephew and the conversation shifted to sports, then to school, and finally, as the evening sky began to darken into the night, they talked about maybe sneaking some of the leftover dinner back out of the refrigerator. They both headed inside.

Binks walked over to the covered food left out on the counter. His wife must have known he would have wanted more food eventually and left it out for him. This thought brought a smile to his face. He put some on a plate for the boy, and some on a plate for himself and they stood there and ate in the kitchen.

"I'll tell you what, your mother can cook a hell of a meal!" Binks said to the boy and the boy nodded his agreement and continued to eat. They cleaned off their plates and then placed them in the sink and headed off to bed after saying goodnight to each other. His wife was already in bed and waiting for him when he opened the door and walked in. He walked over to her and kissed her on the forehead and said, "I'm going to shower and clean up, don't fall asleep on me ok?" to which she responded, "You better hurry up..."

He walked over to the bathroom and passed a stack of papers on top of the dresser. There lay some old love letters he had written her over the years when they had been apart. On the top was a poem he had written her from one of his many deployments. It was very amateur, the last words seemed to rhyme but there was not much structure to it. You don't think about those things when you are in a combat zone writing a love letter, you just write what is in your heart.

Binks picked up the piece of paper that was on the top of the stack and re-read the words he had written her years before…

The pure things in life, get better with time

That's good news for you, reading my terrible rhymes

The flickering flame of passion matures to steady red ember

Happy memories for my mind to look back on and remember

The best things in life get better with time

Like fiery Young love, and dusty Old wine

He smiled. It was cheesy, but the feeling remained the same. He could remember exactly how he had felt when he had penned those words. How the thought of coming home to her gave him hope, and fear at the same time. He wasn't afraid of physical pain and wasn't afraid to die. The thought of death only terrified him when he thought of never being able to touch her again.

He showered and then slid under the covers next to his wife. He pulled her close and kissed the back of her neck. This was his heaven. This was why he did not want to leave tomorrow. Not out of fear for what might happen to him, but for fear that he might not be in this situation again. That was perhaps what made it so precious to him. He knew this could very well be the last time, so he held on tighter and committed every bit of it to his memory. He wondered if other people felt this way, or if it was unique to someone like him, someone who knew how quickly the conscious mind can leave this sack of meat and bones. A candle on the nightstand next to the bed was flickering and casting shadows in a way that reminded him of the illumination rounds that had flickered in Korea on that night.

He held her hand, their fingers interlaced. He observed his calloused hand holding hers and thought about all of the lives that that same calloused hand had ended. Of all the things that his hands were capable of doing, nothing felt as right as holding hers. This is what his hands were meant to do. He wanted to come back home to her, and he had not even left yet. His eyelids felt heavy and he surrendered to the need for sleep and drifted off into the realm of dreams.

The next morning, he loaded his green sea bag into the back of his brother's truck, as they got ready to head to the airport. He felt a tap on his arm and looked down to see that his nephew was at his elbow. The boy's eyes were welling up with tears, and it was clear he was trying his hardest to not let them spill over. The boy didn't say anything. The boy didn't want his mom, who was standing behind him to hear his voice crack as he knew it would if he tried to talk. Binks saw this, and it felt like his heart was torn in half. He bent over and hugged the boy tightly.

"I love you, buddy," Binks said as his own eyes were beginning to well with tears.

He glanced up at his wife who was standing back by the porch and the slight movement of his head caused a tear welling in his eyes to spill over and begin to run down his cheek. She was a strong woman. A good woman. He kissed the top of the boy's head, and then placed his hands on his shoulders and held him at arm's length for a second, and looked into his eyes. Binks could remember being the boy's age. It felt like it was just yesterday, and yet it felt like it was hundreds of years ago.

He walked over to his wife. Her eyes were filling with tears, and as she hugged him, they rolled down her cheek and onto his chest. He gave her one last kiss on the forehead and told her he loved her. Then, he got into the truck and drove away, heading for his last deployment.

Chapter 9

As the truck left the front gate of the house that Binks had grown up in, it took a right turn onto the dirt road that would lead the two miles to the nearest paved road. Binks was riding shotgun, his brother driving. He looked out the passenger side window at his wife and nephew and thought back to the times that he had sped down this road as a young driver and before that, when he had ridden his pedal bicycle down the road as a child.

This road had so many memories attached to it. As a boy, he and his brother had ridden their bikes to the neighboring farms and done work around the places for the older farmers. Binks kept his eyes on the house as it began to disappear into the cloud of dust behind them. He was filled with a deep level of sadness. It was a dead tree of sadness that came from inside of his physical being, but its roots felt much deeper than his body. The sadness seemed to come from a pitch-black hole in the ground with no apparent bottom. It came from the very center of the universe and he felt like he was falling through that hole. As the house disappeared, so too faded the light of his life. He felt so full last night, and so empty now.

It seemed to Binks like human emotion was a zero-sum game. Being with his wife in harmonious situations brought with it the highest of highs, which were inevitably followed by the lowest of lows when their time together ended. Before she had come into Binks life his emotions had held very little variance. It was a flat line mostly with rather small increases of happiness and rather small dips into sadness. Then he had met her. She introduced him to real love and affection. He had never been shown love before in that manner.

In her touch, he had found a new religion. She was everything to him. She had given him such highs emotionally, which were inevitably followed by very low downward swings when he had to leave. The good feelings made the bad worth it. He was a better man for having met her, and every moment he had with her was one that he was truly grateful for. The truck began to slow down. They were approaching the hardtop road. Binks now stared straight out of the windshield at the open land before him. He felt empty.

At the airport, they pulled over and got out. Binks had never been great with emotions, and this was no exception. He looked at his brother and thought about everything they had been through and how grateful he was to have his brother in his life. They shook hands and went into a half hug with three pats on the back and said goodbye. His brother had been through thick and thin with him. Binks hoped that his brother knew how much he loved him, although they had never specifically spoken those words.

After the flight from Kentucky landed in San Diego, he took a cab to Camp Pendleton where he reported back into his unit. He began getting back into the swing of things to get ready for his last deployment before retirement. The next couple of weeks went by in a blur and then, before he knew it, he was on an aircraft headed to FOB Four in Vietnam. Vietnam was a country he had never had any intention of going to, in an area of the world that he had never envisioned himself being again.

The plane landed and he grabbed his pack and filed off the plane with the rest. This was no Korea. Korea had been cold. Way too cold. Vietnam was hot and humid. He was off the plane and on the tarmac for less than a minute and he felt himself starting to perspire.

Binks already hated this place. It was the opposite of Korea in temperature, but it had a familiar feeling in the air. He was flagged down by a young Marine who had been sent to receive him and show him where he was to stay. They walked across the tarmac and through some pop-up tents.

The aura of Vietnam was pure misery. A Marine with his arm in a sling walked by with his sleeves rolled up and blouse unbuttoned. His dead eyes stared into Binks' soul as they passed. Normally, Binks would have stopped and told him to fix his appearance, but for some reason he just stared. Binks had an odd feeling looking into those eyes, so void of life. It made his stomach sink a little. He hadn't seen those eyes on a Marine since Korea. He was back in war.

As he followed the Marine in front of him, he looked around at the other people in the camp. Blouses were undone, bandanas on their heads, weapons hanging every which way that was most comfortable at the moment, and he could feel eyes on him from every direction. With his clean uniform and appearance, he seemed wildly out of place here.

He walked into the tent that was to be his. His role in this war was different from the last one. He was now Explosive Ordinance Disposal and was the head of an EOD section that would be taking care of an Area of Operations that included the range for this FOB and about five other temporary smaller combat outposts that were occupied by infantry or other special operations units.

The days went by and Binks settled into his new routine. The day-to-day operations of life in Vietnam reflected those of Korea in some ways. Complaining about the weather was always a constant gripe everywhere Marines deployed. The same old bitching, just in a new environment.

Binks' main responsibility in the war was rendering explosive ordinances that did not detonate on impact, as safe. He did so by doing controlled detonations using blocks of TNT to blow them up. He did not go on patrols, he just waited until a unit called in on the radio about the ordinance they had, and then he would go there and blow it up safely and predictably.

The base that he was on had a strong defense set up. On the inside, you were relatively safe. What was considered to be the "front line" or the hot zones were several miles away. For this reason, Binks felt comfortable sitting in a relatively open space, watching the sun sink down. There was an evening breeze that was just strong enough to keep the mosquitoes from landing. Just enough to cool you down and rid you of mosquitoes for the moment. Binks loved sunsets, although his wife preferred sunrises. She said she liked the idea of watching a new beginning. The sun rising on a new day. The possibilities of what might happen on that day were endless. Binks was attracted to sunsets. Watching the sun sink over the horizon. The end of a day. There is beauty in graceful endings. To him, it signaled the end of the workday and the beginning of the relaxing night next to a fire or lying next to his woman.

As the sun began to dip behind the horizon Binks closed his eyes and focused on the last rays of sunshine and wind that hit his face. In those moments, when he closed his eyes, he could be anywhere in the world. He lost himself in the moment. The wind slowed down and an insect landed on his neck that brought him back to reality. He slapped it and its' body became a spec of black goo that was split evenly between his neck and left hand. He stood up and made his way back to his quarters.

There was a special operations outpost about 10 miles north of the FOB that Binks got called out to the following day. The outpost had been hit by Viet Cong mortars the previous day and one of the rounds had landed in the center of their camp and had not exploded on impact. Binks took two EOD Marines and a squad of infantry Marines out to the site to do a controlled demolition of the mortar round.

When Binks arrived at the special operations outpost he saw the round stuck nose-down in the ground in the center of the outpost. The fins on the mortar were sticking up into the air. It looked to be structurally sound. *It should be a fairly cut and dry detonation* Binks thought to himself.

Binks instructed his two junior EOD Marines to start cordoning off the area and then he headed to the COC (the Combat Operations Center). The command tent was in the center of the combat outpost and was fortified with sandbags around the outside of the tent, but the top was just a tarp. It was indicative of the amount of time they had to set up the outpost. They didn't have the time or materials to fortify the top of the command tent.

A Marine that was standing there introduced himself as Staff Sgt McCormick and informed Binks of the current situation in the area. They had a few mortar rounds that were dropped in that morning, but nothing since then. Binks and McCormick talked about how long this war might last and what was happening in the area and the country in general, then Binks headed outside and started walking towards the mortar he had been sent to take care of.

He took out some tape and slowly taped two sticks of TNT to the outside of the mortar. Every time he did so he always shot a little prayer to God about how he would prefer to go home and die an old man next to his wife, rather than getting blown up. As he primed into the TNT he thought back to when he was in Korea and how he had talked about wanting to die a warrior's death. It seemed like such an idiotic thing to want in hindsight. He would much rather go home.

He primed into the TNT with a blasting cap. The blasting cap was crimped at the edges around a green tube about 18 inches long that ended at the ignitor. The green tube was filled with a slow-burning material that helped Binks time the detonation of a charge, hence the reason it was known as a time fuse. He taped the cap into place, and then, taped the fuse onto the round as well so there was no risk of the blasting cap moving or the time fuse shifting once he popped the ignitor. Then he stepped back, looked at it, scanned around to make sure the cordon was still clear. He ensured no one was in the blast radius, and popped the pin that started the burning of the time fuse.

"90 Seconds!" He yelled and then walked towards the COC and the cover behind the sandbags it provided.

He stopped when he reached the makeshift doorway and turned back to look at the charge.

Scanning again to make sure no one was walking around and that everyone was behind cover of some sort from the blast.

"60 Seconds!" He yelled.

It was deadly quiet. The sun was just starting to touch the tops of the trees and the evening breeze was picking up again. The absurdity of the beauty and calm of the world in that moment, when Binks knew it was about to be shattered by an explosion, struck him as slightly amusing and a tight-lipped smile crept across his face.

"30 Seconds!" He yelled. He checked to make sure no one was in sight and then stepped fully into the COC for the last few seconds.

"10!"

"5!"

"3!"

"2!"

"1!"

The blast went off right as he yelled out "One!" and a few small chunks of debris rained down on top of the tarp.

Right on time. For a moment he felt relief. He stood up to go check the blast site to make sure that the mortar had properly detonated. As he walked out the entryway of the COC he heard the unmistakable whistle of a large projectile flying overhead. "Incoming!!" He yelled and jumped back into the COC. The blast hit about 100m north of the COC.

"They must have used the mortar det to try to zero in on us!" The radio operator exclaimed and then began chattering into the radio for air support.

Nothing is ever as easy as it could be, Binks thought to himself as he took a knee on the inside of the COC and began to send a silent prayer up to the heavens.

Another round dropped a little over 50 meters South of the COC. They were closing in. A third round dropped in. This one shook the ground and sent shrapnel flying into the sandbags. They were within effective killing range, the only thing that had kept Binks alive was the fact that he had the sandbags between him and where the round just went off. He reached in between the buttons on his blouse and wrapped his hand around the small wooden cross that hung from the necklace his wife had given him.

"Air inbound!" the radio operator stated loudly to the room, and then leaned back into the microphone and stayed on the hook with the spotter who had seen where they were set up at.

An explosion rocked the COC and the shock wave slammed Binks head backward violently and his world went black. For a moment there was nothing but black until his consciousness slowly started to come back to him. His eyes were working hard to focus on what was happening around him. Dirt and debris fell from the sky. He felt wet for some reason. He could feel warm fluid on his chest, thighs, and arms.

His eyes slowly focused on his legs and he could see that the warm fluid was his own blood seeping from his body that had just been ripped open by shrapnel from a mortar.

His ears were ringing, but through the ringing, he could faintly make out the sound of screaming. Binks' eyes finally focused on the thing in front of him. The radio operator was standing on one leg. The operator was staring dumfounded at the lower part of his formerly attached right leg as he held it in his hands.

He tried his hardest to breathe but the heaving of his chest brought no relief. He felt like he was inhaling water. His eyes went wide and a feeling of panic gripped him.

He wanted to see the sun.

He wanted to feel the breeze.

He wanted to hold his wife.

He clutched the flask in his left breast pocket with his right hand. With his left arm dragged himself to the edge of the doorway and propped himself up. Fear of death and a desire to live to see his wife drove him to keep moving despite the excruciating pain. He paused for a second in the doorway. Just for a moment so he could catch his breath.

The sun was starting to touch to tops of the trees to the west, and the evening breeze lightly brushed his face. The same wind that he had felt as a child hunting deer, as a man hunting men in Korea, as a husband sitting next to his wife on the porch back home, he felt it again.

The memory of his wife renewed the panic he had felt before. He was determined not to die so he could make it back to her. Once again, he focused his efforts on getting a full breath of air, and once again it was to no avail. His body wouldn't cooperate. The edges of his vision were beginning to go dark. Through the ringing in his ears he could hear the gurgling noises coming from his chest, mouth, and throat with every breath he struggled to take. Then, he saw her. Such a perfect and beautiful angel. She was walking towards him, coming from the barn. God's gift to him.

She walked up and sat down next to him on the bench. She put her arms around him and gently kissed his cheek and interlaced her fingers on her left hand into the fingers on his right hand. He looked at her beautiful hand inside of his dirty and bloody hand that had taken lives, disposed of bombs, helped his brothers, thrown baseballs, and held his wife. His hand was where it was meant to be, doing what it was meant to do, holding hers. "I am so happy your home," she said. He leaned his head against her.

He felt like he was in heaven.

Manufactured by Amazon.ca
Bolton, ON